Second-Chance Sweet Shop

Rochelle Alers

W9-AZF-319

 HARLEQUIN® SPECIAL EDITION

Recycling programs
for this product may
not exist in your area.

ISBN-13: 978-1-335-89430-4

Second-Chance Sweet Shop

Copyright © 2019 by Rochelle Alers

Printed in U.S.A.

Since 1988, national bestselling author **Rochelle Alers** has written more than eighty books and short stories. She has earned numerous honors, including the Zora Neale Hurston Award, the Vivian Stephens Award for Excellence in Romance Writing and a Career Achievement Award from *RT Book Reviews*. She is a member of Zeta Phi Beta Sorority, Inc., Iota Theta Zeta Chapter. A full-time writer, she lives in a charming hamlet on Long Island. Rochelle can be contacted through her website, www.rochellealers.org.

Books by Rochelle Alers

Harlequin Special Edition

Wickham Falls Weddings

Home to Wickham Falls
Her Wickham Falls SEAL
The Sheriff of Wickham Falls
Dealmaker, Heartbreaker
This Time for Keeps

American Heroes

Claiming the Captain's Baby
Twins for the Soldier

Harlequin Kimani Romance

The Eatons

Sweet Silver Bells
Sweet Southern Nights
Sweet Destiny
Sweet Persuasions
Twice the Temptation
Sweet Dreams
Sweet Deception

Visit the Author Profile page
at Harlequin.com for more titles.

Give her the fruit of her hands; and let her own works praise her in the gates.

Chapter One

The chilly February temperature and lightly falling rain did little to dispel the excitement coursing through Sasha Manning. She'd lost track of the number of times she had glanced at the wall clock. It was a week before Valentine's Day and the grand opening of her patisserie. Sasha's Sweet Shoppe was located on Main Street, in the heart of Wickham Falls' downtown business district. The mayor, several members of the town council and the chamber of commerce had promised to be on hand at ten for the ribbon-cutting photo op.

"You can keep staring at that clock, but it isn't going to make the hands move any faster."

Sasha turned to look at her mother. Charlotte Manning had worked tirelessly alongside her over the past four months to get the shop ready. And Sasha knew Charlotte, who'd had a mild heart attack nearly a year ago, could not continue to put in such long hours. Several days ago, she'd posted a help-wanted sign in the front window.

"I keep wondering if they're going to cancel the photo shoot because of the weather." The words were barely off her tongue when the town's photographer knocked lightly on the door. Sasha pressed her palms together to conceal their trembling. The door chimed when she opened it.

"Good morning, Jonas."

"Good morning, Sasha. Charlotte."

Jonas Harper, performing double duty as the photographer for the town and *The Sentinel*, Wickham Falls' biweekly, set his leather equipment bag on the floor and then walked over to the showcases filled with colorful confectionaries. "They look too pretty to eat."

Sasha smiled at the middle-aged man with a salt-and-pepper ponytail. She'd spent the past two days putting together an assortment of tarts, tortes, cookies and pies. Earlier that morning she'd baked several loaves of white, wheat, rye and pumpernickel bread. "I've put aside samples for you and the others."

Jonas unzipped his bright yellow waterproof poncho. "Is there someplace where I can hang this up?"

Charlotte stepped forward and held out her hand. "I'll take that for you."

Sasha watched her mother as she took Jonas's poncho, offering him a bright smile. At fifty-six, Charlotte was still a very attractive woman, despite what she'd had to go through during her volatile marriage to a man she was never able to please. Her blond hair was now a shimmering silver and there were a few noticeable lines around her bright blue eyes.

As the youngest of three, and the only girl, Sasha would cover her head with a pillow to drown out what were daily arguments between her parents. She had counted down the time until she graduated high school and could leave Wickham Falls, as her brothers had done when they enlisted in the military. It had been more than a decade since she'd called Wickham Falls home, but now she was back to stay.

"This place is really nice," Jonas said, as he glanced around the bakery. "It reminds me of some of the little bakeshops I saw when I visited Paris."

Sasha nodded, smiling. The colorful wallpaper stamped with images of pies, cakes, muffins and cupcakes provided a cheerful backdrop for twin refrigerated showcases, recessed lights, a quartet of pendants, and a trio of bistro tables and chairs. She had also purchased a coffee press, a cappuccino machine and a commercial blender to offer specialty coffees.

"That's what I had in mind when I decided to open this place." Although she'd never been to Paris, she had watched countless televised travel and cooking shows featuring French cooking to know exactly how she wanted her patisserie to look. Her mother had teased her, saying perhaps the residents of The Falls weren't ready for fancy tarts and pastries with names they weren't able to pronounce. But Sasha refused to let anyone dissuade her from her dream of starting over as a successful pastry chef.

When growing up she hadn't known what she wanted to do or be. Everything changed, once she left Wickham Falls and moved to Tennessee to accept a position as a companion to an elderly woman. Adele Harvey, the former English teacher and reclusive widow of a man who made a fortune buying and selling real estate, had become the grandmother Sasha never had.

Sasha saw the ad online for a live-in companion and filled out an application, despite not having any experience aside from occasionally babysitting her neighbors' young children. Two weeks following her high school graduation Sasha boarded a bus for a trip to Memphis, Tennessee, for an in-person interview with Mrs. Harvey and the attorney overseeing the legal affairs of the childless widow. It had taken the older woman only ten minutes to announce she was hired, and when Sasha returned to Memphis in mid-August it was as a first-class passenger on a direct flight, followed by a chauffeur-driven limo to what would become her new home.

The bell chimed again, breaking into her thoughts, and the editor of the newspaper walked in. Langston Cooper had left The Falls to pursue a career as a journalist. For more than a decade he had covered the Middle East as a foreign correspondent for an all-news cable station before returning to the States to write several bestselling books. His life mirrored Sasha's when he married a popular singer, but the union was dissolved amid rumors that she'd had an affair with an actor. Langston returned to Wickham Falls, took over ownership of the dwindling biweekly and within two years had increased the newspaper's circulation and advertising revenue.

Taking off his baseball cap, he smiled at Sasha, exhibiting straight, white teeth in his light brown complexion. Growing up, Langston and her brother had been what folks said were as thick as thieves. You'd never see one without the other.

Walking over to him, she pressed her cheek to his smooth-shaven jaw. "Thank you for coming."

Langston dropped a kiss on the mass of curly hair framing Sasha's round face. "Did you actually think I would miss the grand opening of The Falls' celebrity pastry chef?"

Sasha blushed to the roots of her natural strawberry-blond hair. She'd dyed the bright red strands a nondescript brown following her divorce to avoid attracting the attention of eagle-eyed paparazzi who'd hounded her relentlessly once the word was out that she was no longer married to country-music heartthrob Grant Richards.

"Have you forgotten that I'm not the only celebrity in The Falls?" she teased with a smile. "After all, you are a *New York Times* bestselling author."

Langston nodded. "I didn't come here for you to talk about me, but about you. After photos and the speeches, I'd like you to schedule some time for an interview for *The Sentinel*'s Who's Who column."

Since coming back to The Falls Sasha had discovered her hometown had changed—and for the better. The list of those returning to Wickham Falls to put down roots was growing. Langston had become editor in chief of *The Sentinel*, Seth Collier was now sheriff, and Sawyer Middleton headed the technology department for the Johnson County Public Schools system. And for Sasha it was a no-brainer. The Falls was the perfect place for her to start over with a business where she did not have a competitor.

"Can you call me in a couple of weeks?" she asked.

"You've got it." Langston leaned closer and kissed

her cheek. "Good luck and congratulations," he said as he left.

She hoped the samples she planned to offer those coming into the shop for her grand opening would generate return customers. A nervous smile barely lifted the corners of her mouth when she spied the mayor, several members of the town council and the head of the chamber of commerce through the plate-glass window.

"It's showtime, Natasha," Charlotte whispered.

"Yes, it is, Mama." Her mother was the only one who had refused to call her by her preferred name. When her mother brought her home from the hospital, her three-year-old brother could not pronounce Natasha; he'd begun calling her Sasha and the name stuck. She walked over to the door and opened it.

Sasha let out an audible sigh when the town officials filed out of the shop, each with a small white box, stamped with the patisserie's logo, and filled with miniature samples of red velvet, pumpkin spice, lemon-lime and chocolate hazelnut cupcakes. Cupcakes had become her signature specialty.

She pushed her hands into the pockets of the pink tunic with her name and the shop's logo stamped over her heart. "Even though Mayor Gillespie was a little long-winded, I think it went well."

"It went very, very well," Charlotte said in agreement. "Jonas took wonderful shots of the shop, and after your interview with Langston I'm willing to bet that you won't be able to keep up with the demand for your cupcakes."

Charlotte gave her daughter a reassuring smile. When she had come back six months before she had felt like crying when she opened the door to see her last born appear to be a shadow of the young woman who had come to her father's funeral what now seemed so long ago. The bright red hair was a mousy brown, and she had lost a lot of weight. At five-nine she'd appeared almost emaciated and it took Charlotte all her resolve not to become hysterical. It was only after she revealed the circumstances behind her marriage and subsequent divorce that Charlotte understood what Natasha had gone through.

Sasha pulled her lower lip between her teeth. She wanted to sell not only cupcakes, but also specialty cakes, breads and made-to-order elegant desserts. Wickham Falls wasn't Nashville, but she didn't plan to offer the small-town residents creations of a lesser quality than those in the Music City. The doorbell chimed and within minutes there was a steady stream of curious potential customers. She'd sold out of fresh bread before the noon hour.

"May I help you?" Sasha asked an attractive teenage girl with large dark brown eyes and neatly braided hair ending at her shoulders.

"Yes. I've come to apply for the part-time counter-person position."

"Are you still in school?"

"Yes, ma'am. I'm finished with my classes at noon, so I'm available from one on."

Sasha didn't want to write the girl off before she interviewed her, although she would've preferred someone more mature. "What's your name?"

"Kiera Adams. My dad is Dwight Adams," she said proudly.

The moment Kiera mentioned her father's name

Sasha realized she was the daughter of the local dentist. "Does your father know you're applying for the position?" She had asked the question because she did not want to have a problem with parents questioning the number of hours their son or daughter were committed to work.

Kiera shook her head. "Not yet. I figured I'd tell him once you hired me."

Sasha bit back a smile. The young woman did not lack confidence. "Mama, could you please cover the front while I talk to Miss Adams?"

Charlotte nodded. "Of course."

Sasha led Kiera to the rear of the shop, where she had set up an area for her office. She glanced over her shoulder. "Please sit down, Kiera. I've made up an application and I'll give you time to fill it out before we talk."

The help-wanted sign had been in the window for three days, and Kiera was the first person to respond. Sasha frosted several dozen cupcakes while Kiera filled out the application.

"I'm finished with the application, Miss..."

"You may call me Sasha," she said when Kiera's words trailed off.

She took the single sheet of paper from the teenager's outstretched hand. It took less than a minute to review what Kiera had written. Although Sasha hadn't included a category for age, Kiera indicated she was sixteen and a junior at the local high school. She was available to work every day beginning at one in the afternoon, and all day Saturday. Her prior work experience was as a temporary receptionist the previous summer at her father's dental practice.

Sasha revealed, if hired, what Kiera would be responsible for. She would need Kiera to work four hours every afternoon from Tuesday through Friday. And if needed, one or two Saturdays each month. "If I hire you, will it interfere with your studies?"

"No, ma'am. Even though I'm enrolled as a junior, I'm taking senior-level classes." She flashed a demure smile. "I took a lot of AP courses when I went to school in New York."

It was apparent Dr. Adams's daughter was very bright, and it was the third time Kiera had referred to her as "ma'am," which made her feel much older than thirty-two. "You are the first one to apply for the position, and I'm going to keep your application on hand. I plan to wait a few more days, and if no one else applies, then I'll contact you. Please keep in mind if I do decide to bring you on that initially you'll start at the minimum wage."

Kiera stood up. "Does that mean I'll get the job?"

Sasha felt as if she'd been just put on the spot. "I'm going to be up-front with you, Kiera. You're still a student and I don't want you to compromise your grades. And because of this I'd like your permission to talk to your father."

Kiera tucked several braids behind one ear. "I don't mind, Miss Sasha." She paused. "Will you call me if you decide not to hire me?"

"I will send you an email."

Leaning down, Kiera picked up her backpack. "Thank you."

Sasha smiled. "You're very welcome. I still have a few samples on hand I'd like to give you from our grand opening. Are you allergic to chocolate?"

A smile spread across the girl's face, softening her

youthful features. "Thank goodness, no. I love chocolate."

Sasha scrunched up her nose. "It's my weakness, too."
She walked over to a refrigerator in the prep kitchen
and took out a candy cane–striped box and filled it with
chocolate crinkle cookies, brownies, a cup of chocolate
mousse topped with whipped cream and grated chocolate, and the last chocolate hazelnut cupcake. "Enjoy.
And thank you for coming in."

Kiera's smile was dazzling. "Thank you so much,
Miss Sasha."

There was something about Kiera's youthful enthu-
siasm Sasha liked.

Dwight Adams's head popped up when he heard the
light tapping on the door to his office. He had a two-
hour wait before seeing his next patient. He hadn't expected to see his daughter until later that night, but her
coming to his practice was a welcome surprise. He came
around the desk to hug her as she dropped the backpack
filled with books on the carpet and set a red-and-white-
striped box on a side table.

"What are you doing here?"

Kiera rose on tiptoe to kiss her father's cheek. "What
happened to 'nice seeing you'?"

"Of course I'm happy to see you. It's just that I didn't
expect you to come here instead of going home. And,
by the way, how did you get here?"

"I asked Grammie to drop me off. She has a luncheon
meeting with the Ladies Auxiliary."

Dwight studied the teenager who was the mirror
image of her mother at that age. The exception was her
complexion and height, which she had inherited from

him. Kiera, at five-six, was four inches taller than her petite five-foot-two mother. The school bus picked up and dropped off Kiera at the house; Dwight's widowed mother lived in a two-bedroom guesthouse Dwight had built on the property.

Kiera rested her hands on the thighs of her denim-covered jeans. "I applied for a part-time job at the new bakery."

Dwight went completely still. "You did what?"

"Please don't lose it, Daddy."

Extending his legs, he ran a hand over his face. "I'm not losing it, Kiera. I just need to know why you feel the need to get a job when you should be concentrating on your schoolwork. And it can't be about money, because I give you an allowance."

Kiera slipped her right hand in her father's left, threading their fingers together. "I need something to beef up my college applications, either work or community service. A lot of kids at school have already signed up at the church, town hall and other businesses in Wickham Falls. And besides, Miss Sasha said I was the first one to apply, so there is a good chance she might hire me."

"What about your working here?" Dwight questioned.

The summer before Kiera had worked for him when the permanent receptionist went on vacation. As a divorced father, he shared custody with his ex-wife, Adrienne; for years Kiera lived in New York with her and spent one month every summer with him in The Falls. He had made it a practice to visit his daughter several times a year, and whenever he returned home, he'd experienced a modicum of guilt that he bore some responsibility for ending his marriage when he'd been away in the military, which resulted in his not being there to see his daughter grow up. However, everything had changed this past summer when Kiera announced she did not want to return to New York to live with her mother and stepfather, and preferred spending the last two years of high school living with her father and grandmother in Wickham Falls.

Dwight had a lengthy conversation with his ex-wife and convinced her it was time for him to have his daughter for more than a month or a brief visit on school holidays. She finally agreed, with the provision that Kiera vacationed with her during the month of July. Assuming the role as a full-time father had also impacted his obligation as an army reservist. Serving his country for almost two decades while attaining the rank of major was now relegated to his past.

"That's nepotism, Daddy. I can't put down that I worked for Dwight Adams, DDS, and not have someone question our relationship. Miss Sasha said she wanted to talk to you beforehand if she decides to hire me. I guess she doesn't want my having a job to mess with my grades."

"Good for her." Dwight liked the idea that Kiera's potential employer was concerned about her education.

Although he was five or six years old than Sasha Manning, Dwight hadn't had much interaction with her when growing up in The Falls. He and two of her older brothers had attended high school at the same time. But he'd heard a lot about Sasha when she became a celebrity chef and then married platinum-selling country singer Grant Richards. He was as surprised as most in town when she returned to The Falls to set up a bakeshop in one of the vacant stores at the far end of Main Street.

Kiera pointed to the box. "She gave me samples of chocolate desserts. I was going to leave it in the break room until I remembered Miss Chambers is on a diet and doesn't want to eat anything with sugar, so I'm going to take them home for Gram…" Her words trailed off when her cell phone rang. Reaching into her jacket pocket, she stared at the phone. "It's Miss Sasha. She said she would email me if she wasn't going to hire me."

Dwight pointed to Kiera's death grip on the small instrument. "Are you going to answer your phone?" He noticed her expression of apprehension when she put it to her ear. Her expression changed quickly as she covered her mouth with her free hand. "Yes. My dad is here with me." Kiera extended the phone to him. "Miss Sasha would like to speak to you."

He took the phone. "Hello."

"Dr. Adams, this is Sasha Manning. Your daughter applied for a part-time position at my bakeshop. Although I told her that I'm waiting to interview other folks, I've decided to hire her, and I would like to talk to you because I need your reassurance that her hours won't conflict with her schoolwork."

Dwight smiled. His priority for his daughter was maintaining her grades so she could gain acceptance into at least one or two of her colleges of choice. It was apparent Sasha was of like mind. They discussed the details of the position. Dwight agreed to let her take the job but warned that if her grades slipped, she'd have to quit.

"I understand that, Dr. Adams. If it's all right with you, I'd like her to start tomorrow. I'm going to need

a copy of her immunizations because she'll be working in what we call food service, and her Social Security number."

"I can get those to you later this afternoon after my
last patient. What time do you close?"

"I draw the shades once I close at six, but I'll be here
later than that. Does that work for you?"

Dwight nodded although she couldn't see him. "Yes."
He was scheduled to see his last patient at 5:30. Then
he would have to go home and get the documents Sasha
needed to place Kiera on her payroll. "I'll probably see
you after you close."

"I'll be here." There came a pause before Sasha's
voice came through the earpiece again. "Thank you,
Dr. Adams. I hope you don't mind my saying, but your
daughter is a delight."

Dwight stared at Kiera staring back at him and
winked at her. He had to agree with Sasha. There was
never a time when he did not enjoy spending time with
his daughter. And now that she was living with him,
they had grown even closer. "I know I sound biased, but
I have to agree with you. She is pretty special."

"I'll see you tonight?"

"Yes," Dwight confirmed.

"Dr. Adams, can you spare a few minutes of your
time when you come because I'd like to talk to you
about something other than your daughter's employment."

He paused, wondering what it was Sasha wanted to
discuss with him. "Yes," Dwight repeated, now that she
had aroused his curiosity. He ended the call and handed
the phone back to Kiera. "It looks as if you're hired."

Kiera clasped her hands together in a prayerful gesture. "When do I start?"

"Tomorrow."

"Instead of the bus dropping me off at the house, I'll get off with some of the other kids on the other side of the tracks."

Dwight nodded. The railroad tracks ran through the downtown business district. "What about lunch?" He knew Kiera left school early because lunch was her last period of the school day.

"I get out at twelve and by the time the bus drops me off it will be about 12:30. Instead of going home to eat, I'll ask Grammie to help me make lunch and I'll eat it here before walking down to the bakery."

He smiled. "You have it all figured out, don't you?"

"Daddy, aren't you the one who told me to have a strategy before I execute a plan?"

Dwight managed to look sheepish. "Yes, I did." He'd lost track of the number of forewarnings he'd given his daughter over the years, and it was apparent she remembered most of them because she could repeat them verbatim.

Dwight found a parking spot behind the bakery and walked around to the front. He'd dropped Kiera at home and told his mother not to plan for him to eat dinner with her and his daughter. He had no way of knowing how long his meeting with Sasha would take.

The woven shade on Sasha's storefront had been pulled down, as had the one covering the front door.

Dwight tapped lightly on a square of the door's beveled glass insert, and seconds later he saw Sasha as she pushed aside the shade and then opened the door. He was just as shocked as many in the town at the word that Sasha Manning was back in town, and without her superstar country-artist husband. She'd kept a low profile until the town council approved her opening a bakeshop in the downtown business district. Questions about her marriage were finally answered when a photographer captured photos of Grant Richards with a woman who was purported to be his new girlfriend. And when reporters asked Grant about his relationship with Sasha, he'd admitted it was over.

Smiling, Sasha opened the door wider. "Please come in."

Chapter Two

Sasha successfully smothered a gasp when she greeted Dwight Adams. He was more than gorgeous. He was beautiful. His balanced features in a lean sable-brown sculpted face, large dark penetrating eyes and dimpled smile were mesmerizing. His buzz-cut salt-and-pepper hair was a shocking contrast to his unlined face. Dressed entirely in black—sheep-lined leather bomber jacket, pullover sweater, jeans and Doc Martens—he was unequivocally the epitome of tall, dark and handsome.

Six years his junior, she'd had little or no interaction with him when growing up. By the time she entered the first grade Dwight was already in middle school. Even if they had been the same age, they might not have traveled in the same circles. Wickham Falls, like so many small towns, was defined by social and economic division. His family lived in an enclave of The Falls populated by those who were middle- and upper-middle-class professionals and business owners, while she had always thought of her family as the working poor, because her father always said he was one paycheck away from the poorhouse. Despite Harold's claim they were poor, Sasha never felt as if they were. Her parents owned their house, there was always food on the table and, as the only girl, she hadn't had to wear hand-me-downs.

She'd overheard some of the girls that were in her brothers' classes whisper about how gorgeous Dwight was, but talking about cute boys or fantasizing about teen idols with her girlfriends had not been reality for Sasha. She'd never wanted to host a sleepover, because what happened in the Manning house stayed within the Manning household. Neither she nor her brothers ever publicly spoke about their parents' toxic union.

What she had never been able to understand was why her parents had married in the first place because they could not agree on anything; and yet they'd celebrated their thirtieth wedding anniversary. Two days later her father passed away from a massive coronary. He was only forty-nine. That was seven years ago, and the first time Sasha had returned to The Falls since leaving at eighteen.

"Congratulations, Sasha. You managed to add some class to The Falls," Dwight said as he glanced around the bakeshop.

She forced a smile she did not quite feel. She had spent more than a year planning to open a bakeshop, several months awaiting the town council's approval, and then even more time until the contractor finished renovating the space to make it functional for her to furnish it with prep tables, sinks, industrial ovens, mixers, blenders, deep fryers, food processors, bakeware and utensils.

"You don't think it's too fancy?"

Dwight turned and met her eyes. "Of course not. It's charming and very inviting." He smiled. "And I like the alliteration of Sasha's Sweet Shoppe."

She nodded. "It took me a while to come up with a catchy name. My first choice was Sasha's Patisserie, but changed my mind because I didn't want to have to explain to folks what a patisserie is."

Dwight walked over to the showcase and peered at the colorfully decorated and labeled pastries. "All they have to say is 'I want one of these and two of those.' By the way, how was your grand opening?"

Sasha moved over to stand next to him. "It went well enough. I gave out a lot of samples, and hopefully it will be enough to induce folks to come back again."

Dwight gave Sasha a sidelong glance. He had been more familiar with her brothers than their little sister. It wasn't until she had become a contestant in a televised baking competition that he, like most living in The Falls, tuned in to watch and remotely cheer her on. The camera appeared to make love to the tall, slender pastry chef with a wealth of red-gold curls, sparkling green eyes and an infectious laugh. Although she did not win the competition, her appearance was enough to make her a viewer favorite. Her star continued to rise when she became the personal baker to several celebrities and married a popular country singer, and then without warning walked away from the bright lights to come back to her place of birth.

It only took a quick glance for Dwight to notice lines of tension around Sasha's mouth. As someone responsible for managing his own practice, he suspected she was apprehensive about making her new business a success.

"I don't think you have anything to worry about. I ate a piece of your chocolate-and-pecan cheesecake and wanted more."

Sasha flashed a relaxed smile for the first time. The gesture softened her mouth as her eyes sparkled like polished emeralds. "I'll definitely put that on my cheesecake list."

Dwight reached into the pocket of his jacket and took out an envelope. "I brought you a copy of Kiera's immunizations and her Social Security number."

Sasha took the envelope. "Come with me. I'm going to scan both and then give them back to you. The less paper I have to file, the better."

He followed her to the rear of the shop, where a spacious immaculate commercial kitchen was outfitted with industrial appliances. His gaze was drawn to a built-in refrigerator/freezer, and then to dozens of cans and labeled jars of spices stacked on metal shelves that spanned an entire wall. Sasha had set up a desk with a computer, printer and file cabinet next to the exit door leading out to the rear parking lot. Bills and invoices were tacked to the corkboard with colorful pushpins affixed to the wall above the desk.

"So, this is where the magic happens."

Sasha nodded, smiling. "Disney may take offense, but this *is* my magic kingdom." She sat on the office chair in front of the computer and patted the straight-back chair next to the workstation. "Please sit down."

"When did you know you wanted to be a baker?" Dwight asked, as he sat where Sasha had indicated.

She swiveled on her chair to face him. "I never wanted to be a baker."

His eyebrows rose slightly. "But don't you bake?"

"Bakers make pies, while pastry chefs make desserts."

Dwight inclined his head. "I apologize and stand corrected." Sasha's low, sensual laugh caressed his ear.

"There's no need to apologize, Dr. Adams."

He gave her a pointed look. "It's Dwight. I'm only Dr. Adams at my office."

Sasha paused and then nodded. A beat passed. "Okay, Dwight. I suppose you're wondering what else I wanted to talk to you about?"

Dwight, sitting with his hands sandwiched between his knees, watched as Sasha inserted a thumb drive into a port. "I must admit I am curious." The seconds ticked as she saved what she'd scanned and handed the papers back to him.

"How difficult was it for you to set up your practice here in The Falls? And how long did it take before you knew it would be viable?"

Her query caught Dwight slightly unawares. He thought Sasha would've established a detailed business plan before deciding to open the shop. After all, she was selling goods that relied on supply and demand, while he offered a specific service.

"Well, it was somehow different for me because there was no dental office in The Falls. I remember my mother complaining about having to drive to Mineral Springs and sit for hours to be seen because the office was always overcrowded and overbooked. And once they added an orthodontist it became bedlam in the waiting room with kids falling over one another. Once I decided I wanted to be a dentist I knew beforehand that I would set up a practice here."

"How long have you had your practice?" Sasha asked.

"This coming October will be eight years."

"Did you know the first year that you would have enough patients to sustain your practice?"

"I knew that only when my patients returned for their sixth-month checkup. My mother was semiretired, so she filled in as my receptionist until I was able to find a permanent one, and after I hired a hygienist, I didn't have to micromanage, and everything fell into place. A couple of months ago I added a dental assistant to our staff who performs some of the duties the hygienist had assumed. Initially, most of my patients were kids who needed to have their teeth checked for school, a few for sleepaway camp, and then after a while I was able to sign up their parents."

"What about your hours?"

"At one time they varied because I was in the reserves and had to serve one weekend a month and two weeks during the summer. I resigned my commission last summer once Kiera came to live with me. Currently, I'm open Mondays and Fridays nine to six, and Tuesdays and Thursdays from one to seven. Even though I no longer go on maneuvers for the two weeks, I still close the office."

"What happened to Wednesdays and Saturdays?"

"Wednesday is designated golf day for doctors even

though I don't golf," he admitted, smiling, "and because I have two late nights, I can spend Saturdays and Sundays with my daughter."

Sasha inhaled a deep breath, held it before slowly exhaling. "I debated whether to close for one day, and then decided on two because I don't have an assistant. Mama had a mild heart attack last year and her cardiologist has cautioned her about overtiring herself. She's been working nonstop helping me to get this place ready, but by afternoons she's so tired that she must get off her feet. Most nights she's in bed by the time I get home. I wanted to wait to see how many more would apply for the part-time afternoon position before I made a decision, but because Kiera was the first to come in, I decided not to prolong the process."

"What time do you come in?" Dwight questioned.

"I get in around six and I'm usually here a couple of hours after closing."

He whistled softly. "That's a long day." Sasha nodded. "I really understand your apprehension, but this isn't the first time you've gone into business for yourself." He wanted to remind her that she had earned the reputation as a celebrity chef.

"That's true, but the difference is I'd worked out of my home and only when I was commissioned to design cakes for special occasions. I'm not questioning my ability as a pastry chef, but whether folks in town are willing to spend money on freshly made baked goods."

Dwight curbed the urge to reach out and take Sasha's hand when he noticed its trembling. "You're experiencing what every other start-up business faces. We don't know how it's going to turn out except that we must take the risk and hope we'll be successful. I had to withdraw money from an annuity to buy machines and equipment to set up the office, and it took me three years before I was able to put it back."

Sasha suddenly felt as if she was being a Negative Nelly. Unlike Dwight, she didn't have to borrow money to set up the bakeshop. She'd earned enough money from designing cakes for A-list celebrities to become financially comfortable, and she'd also inherited a small fortune from her former employer. Luckily, she'd signed a prenup before marrying Grant with the stipulation he wasn't entitled to her earnings, just as she wasn't entitled to what he'd received from his recording contracts. She'd had Adele Harvey to thank for the advice as to how she should protect her money.

"I'm sorry to bend your ear about…"

"Stop it, Sasha," Dwight said softly, cutting her off. "There's no need to apologize. You're not the first and won't be the last person to experience preopening jitters. I'm willing to bet you'll have a line out the door like the ones in Brooklyn when folks order cakes from Junior's for Thanksgiving and Christmas."

Her expression brightened noticeably. "You know about Junior's?"

Grinning from ear to ear, Dwight chuckled softly. "One of my army buddies was a native New Yorker and he knew every popular eating spot on Long Island and the five boroughs. The first time he took me to Junior's for dinner and suggested I try the cheesecake, I was hooked. I try to visit Junior's at least once every time I go to New York."

"Do you go often?"

"I used to go back three or four times a year when Kiera lived with my ex-wife."

The mention of an ex-wife had Sasha wondering if Dwight had remarried, despite his not wearing a wedding band. However, his marital status was of no import to her at the moment. Her sole focus was making a go of her patisserie.

"After I graduated from culinary school, I took a two-month break and treated myself to trips to DC, New York and Boston to visit a number of restaurants who'd earned a reputation for their signature desserts. Junior's was on my list for cheesecakes once I got to New York City. Everything I'd heard or read about their cheesecakes could not accurately describe what I'd eaten. I'd become so obsessed in attempting to duplicate their recipe that I gave up and now use a basic recipe and slightly tweak it to make it my own."

"Your cheesecake is spectacular."

A rush of heat suffused her face. "Thank you."

Dwight stretched out long legs and crossed his arms over his chest. "You can count me as a regular customer if you send me an email whenever you bake bagels, ciabatta, focaccia, cinnamon raisin or Irish soda bread."

Sasha felt a rush of excitement for the first time since sitting down with Dwight. She was looking forward to foot traffic for special-order items. "I'll definitely add your name to my mailing list. I plan to alert everyone on the list of the day's special." She pushed to her feet, Dwight rising with her, and extended her hand. "Thank you for the pep talk. I left a pad at the front of the shop for you to put down your contact information."

Dwight took her hand, his larger one closing over

her fingers. He went completely still. "Why is your hand so cold?"

"I've always had cold hands."

"Cold hands, warm heart?" he teased.

"You've got it," Sasha countered.

Once her marriage soured and she felt comfortable enough to disclose the details to her mother, Charlotte had accused her of loving with her heart rather than her head. She didn't want to tell the older woman that she did not want a repeat of her marriage, where every day was filled with hostility, so she'd bitten her tongue in order to keep the peace. However, in the end she knew she could not continue to put up with a man who was continually threatened that her popularity was surpassing his, as he constantly reminded her. It had taken more than six months for her to finally tell Grant it was over and that she wanted out. Much to her surprise, he agreed, and less than a year later they went their separate ways.

Dwight increased his hold on her hand, his thumb caressing the back and adding warmth not only to her fingers but adding a rush of warmth through her whole body. Though undeniably innocent, the motion elicited shivers of sensual awareness coursing through her. Sasha could not believe she was reveling in the feel of a man holding her hand.

"May I please have my hand back?" A teasing smile tilted the corners of her mouth.

Dwight dropped it as if it was a venomous snake. "Sorry about that."

I'm not, Sasha thought. She wasn't sorry because it had been much too long since she'd found herself affected by a man's touch. Now that she looked back on her relationship with her ex-husband, Sasha knew she had been in denial when she refused to see what had been so apparent from her first date with Grant. He was a narcissist. It had to be all about him.

Despite what she'd felt when Dwight held her hand, Sasha knew there was no way she could allow herself to be swayed by romantic fantasies. Her sole focus was making certain she remained in business. She had invested too much time and money in the bakeshop to have it fail. Dwight stared at her, and suddenly she felt like a specimen on a slide under a microscope.

Without warning, a wave of exhaustion washed over her as she tried unsuccessfully to stifle a yawn. "It has been a long day, and as soon as I let you out, I'm going to head home. I'd planned to put up a batch of dough for bread, but that's something I'll do when I come in early tomorrow."

"I'll wait and walk you out."

Sasha shook her head. "Thank you for offering, but I believe I can find my way to the parking lot rather easily."

"I'll still wait and walk you to your car."

"If you say so."

"I do."

There was something in Dwight's voice that indicated no matter what she said she wouldn't be able to dissuade him. She showed him where he could put down his contact information before returning to the kitchen to turn off lights and retrieve her tote from the lower drawer in the file cabinet. Dwight met her as she armed the security system, opened and locked the rear door behind them.

Sasha pointed to the van parked several spaces down

from the bakeshop. The parking lot was brightly lit with newly installed high-intensity streetlamps. A rash of burglaries and break-ins had prompted shopkeepers to get the town council to approve improved lighting to protect their businesses.

"The white van is mine."

Dwight walked her to her vehicle and waited for her to unlock the doors. "Do you want to give me a hint about tomorrow's special?"

"Red velvet cheesecake brownies. I'll put aside a few and give them to Kiera when she comes in. One of the perks will be she will get samples of the day's special." Dwight's dimples reminded Sasha of the indentations in thumbprint cookies when he smiled.

"That sounds like a plan."

Sasha got in behind the wheel and started up the van. "Get home safe," she said before closing the door. Dwight hadn't moved as she put the vehicle in Reverse and drove out of the lot. Talking to him had offered Sasha a modicum of confidence that she could have a successful business offering the residents of Wickham Falls fresh baked goods.

Ten minutes later, she maneuvered into the driveway of the three-bedroom house where she'd grown up, and where her mother still lived. It wasn't until she'd returned to The Falls and moved back in the house that she'd realized how small it was. Eleven hundred square feet was a far cry from the six-thousand-square-foot home she'd shared with her husband in Nashville's tony West End neighborhood. Sitting on three acres of prime real estate, the house was so large the builder had installed intercoms for her to communicate with Grant whenever they were in opposite wings of the mansion.

Sasha had given all of it up—the guitar-shaped in-ground pool, the horses she'd loved to ride, and rubbing shoulders with Nashville's country royalty—in order to control her destiny. The first night she crawled into the bed in her childhood bedroom, she slept for twelve uninterrupted hours and woke feeling as if she had been reborn. It took two months for her to put together a business plan to start over in a town she'd fled fourteen years before. Not only had she changed; the family dynamics had also changed. Her father was gone, and her brothers were lifers in the military, which left just her and her mother.

She parked the van beside Charlotte's brand-new Corolla. Sasha had purchased the vehicle as a birthday gift a week after returning to The Falls, because her mother's car had spent more time in the garage than it had on the road. She ignored Charlotte's complaint that she didn't need a new car, now that she was retired, and that a used one would suffice. Sasha had had to remind the older woman that she was entitled to own a vehicle that hadn't belonged to someone else first.

She got out, unlocked the front door, walked into the house and was met with mouthwatering aromas wafting to her nose. "Mama, I'm home," Sasha called out as she dropped her tote on a bench seat and left her shoes on the mat inside the door.

Charlotte came out of the kitchen wearing her ubiquitous bibbed apron. Sasha could not remember a time when her mother did not wear an apron when cooking. "I thought you were coming home much later."

Sasha ran her hand through the curls falling over her forehead. "I changed my mind."

"Are you feeling all right?"

She registered the concern in Charlotte's voice. "I'm just a little tired." The apprehension coupled with euphoria she'd felt earlier that morning had dissipated like air leaking out of a balloon. "I'm going to eat with you, then take a long soak in the tub before going to bed."

"Did you talk to Dr. Adams?" Charlotte asked.

Sasha smiled. "Yes. He gave me the papers I need to put Kiera on the payroll. I asked him about him setting up his dental practice, and he gave me some good advice. He also promised to become a steady customer if I bake some of his favorite breads."

Charlotte wrapped an arm around Sasha's waist. "Come. We'll talk in the kitchen. I still have to whip up the mashed potatoes."

Sasha sniffed the air. "You made meat loaf." Her mother nodded. Charlotte knew meat loaf with mashed potatoes was her favorite comfort food. There had been a time when as a wife and mother Charlotte made it a practice to make her husband and children's favorite dishes once a week. For Sasha it was meat loaf. Fried chicken for her brother Philip, grilled pork chops for Stephen and beef stew for her father.

"Yes. And it's time I take it out of the oven." Reaching for an oven mitt, Charlotte opened the eye-level oven and set the hot pan on a trivet.

"I'm going to wash my hands, and then I'll finish the potatoes," Sasha volunteered.

"Are you sure?" Charlotte asked.

"Yes. Sit down and put your feet up."

She did not want to remind her mother that she had been up before dawn and needed at least eight to ten hours of sleep to keep up her stamina. But Sasha hoped things would change with her new hire. Now Charlotte would be able to leave the shop midday and return home to rest before starting dinner.

"I'm not an invalid," Charlotte argued softly, as she opened the refrigerator and took out a bowl of Greek salad and a cruet with dressing.

"I know that, Mama. But remember what the doctor said about overtiring yourself. You have a follow-up medical checkup next month and I know you're looking forward to good news."

"I am. But I feel more like a toddler than a grandmother having to take naps in the afternoon."

Married at eighteen, Charlotte had delivered Philip at nineteen, and he, following in his mother's footsteps, married within days of graduating high school. He made Charlotte a grandmother before her fortieth birthday.

"You'll be back to your former self when you least expect it."

After laying out another place setting, Charlotte sat down. She smiled. "That's what I'm hoping. And what about you, Natasha?"

Sasha halted washing her hands in one of the twin sinks. "What about me, Mama?"

"Do you resent having to come back to The Falls after living the high life in Nashville?"

Sasha went completely still before reaching for a paper towel to dry her hands. "Why would you ask me that?"

Charlotte shrugged under a flower-sprigged blouse. The tiny blue flowers were an exact match for her eyes. "There are times when I see so much sadness in your eyes that I believe you'd rather be somewhere else."

Pushing her hands into a pair of oven mitts, Sasha picked up the pot of boiled potatoes and emptied it into a large colander, steam temporarily clouding her vision. "If I'd wanted to be somewhere else, I never would've come home."

"I hope you didn't come back for me."

Sasha closed her eyes for several seconds as she carefully chose her words. She didn't know what had triggered her mother to question her motive for returning to her hometown. "I came back for me *and* you, Mama. I was so sick of the so-called high life that there were days when I didn't want to get out of bed. There was a time when I couldn't wait to leave The Falls, and then fast-forward fourteen years and I couldn't wait to come back. My only concerns are you getting well and making certain the bakeshop will be successful. When I mentioned my apprehension to Dwight, he reassured me what I'm feeling is normal for anyone opening a new business."

"I'm surprised he's going to allow his daughter to work for you."

"Why would you say that?"

"Everyone knows he's very protective of that girl. That's probably the reason why he hasn't remarried."

"How long has he been divorced?"

"Kiera may have been in the second grade when his wife left him."

Charlotte mentioning Dwight's marital status stirred Sasha's curiosity about the attractive dentist. "Why did they break up?" She riced the potatoes, added milk, unsalted melted butter, garlic powder, fresh chives, and then whisked the mixture until it was smooth and fluffy.

"I don't know if there's any truth to it, but folks were saying Adrienne didn't want him to set up a practice in

Wickham Falls and she gave him an ultimatum. In the end, she left, and he stayed."

"But didn't she know when she married him that he didn't want to leave The Falls?" Sasha asked. There were very few people in town Charlotte wasn't familiar with. After thirty years as a cafeteria worker for Johnson County Public Schools, she had come to know every student from kindergarten through twelfth grade during her tenure.

"I don't know. The only thing I can say is the Wheelers spoiled Adrienne because she was the only girl in a family with four boys, and with her looks she knew she could have any boy she wanted. And once she set her sights on Dwight it was all she wrote. Would you mind if I open a bottle of that fancy wine you sent me?" Charlotte asked, changing the topic of conversation. "After all, we are celebrating your grand opening, and there are a few bottles chilling in the fridge."

"You're right about that, Mama." Once Grant went on an extended ten-city tour, Sasha had shipped her clothes, wine collection and personal possessions to Wickham Falls. She had become quite the wine connoisseur once she learned to pair those which complemented fish, red meat and poultry. "Red or champagne?"

"Champagne."

Before moving to Tennessee, Sasha rarely had mother-daughter dates, but since returning, she had come to see another side of Charlotte's personality. As a young wife and mother, Charlotte had sought to shield her children from her husband's temper tantrums, while taking the brunt of his constant bitching and moaning about how much he hated his job as an orderly at the county hospital. Sasha expertly removed the cork from the bottle and filled two flutes with the pale bubbly wine. She touched her glass to Charlotte's. "A toast to Sasha's Sweet Shoppe."

Charlotte smiled. "Hear, hear!"

Between sips of champagne, bites of succulent meat loaf and garlic-infused mashed potatoes, she felt completely relaxed for the first time since getting out of bed earlier that morning. And once she recalled the events of the day, Sasha knew her grand opening had been a rousing success.

She peered over the flute at the updated kitchen. When she'd returned to Wickham Falls for her father's funeral, it was as if she saw the kitchen and bathrooms in the house where she'd grown up for the first time. Had they always been that outdated, or was she comparing them to the ones in the ultramodern mansion she'd shared with her then-husband?

Charlotte refused to accept money for the renovations, so Sasha contacted a local contractor and had him send her plans to redo the kitchen, full bath and the half bath off the mudroom. When the contracting crew showed up to begin work, her mother called and read her the riot act. Sasha hung up, waited a week and then called Charlotte back. She could not stop talking about how much she loved her new kitchen.

The money for the renovations hadn't come from what she'd earned as a pastry chef, but from an account Adele Harvey's financial manager had established for her following the older woman's death. No one was more shocked than Sasha when she had been summoned to the reading of Adele's will and informed she'd been left enough money to take her into old age, if she didn't squander it.

After her second glass of champagne, Sasha was unable to smother a yawn. "As soon as I help you clean up the kitchen, I'm going upstairs to take a bath and then turn in for the night."

Charlotte touched the napkin to the corners of her mouth. "You don't have to help me. I took a nap this afternoon, so I'm good."

Sasha stared across the table at her mother. She'd styled her hair in a becoming bob that showed her delicate features to their best advantage. Although she'd been widowed for seven years, Charlotte had never spoken about dating or the possibility of marrying again. However, it was different with Sasha. At thirty-two, she hoped she would find someone with whom she could fall in love, marry and have one or two children. Thankfully being married to Grant had not turned her off of marriage as a whole. If or when she did decide to date again, she was certain to be cognizant of the signs she'd chosen to ignore with Grant. She had been so blinded by love that she'd surrendered her will and had permitted her husband to control her very existence.

He had insisted she travel with him whenever he was on tour, attend his recording sessions and of course all the televised award shows. She had smiled pretty for the camera even if they'd had an argument earlier that night. After a while Sasha had had enough and decided she wanted out.

Here in The Falls, she did not have to concern herself about being dressed just so or going out without makeup to conceal her freckles. It had taken her living in a plastic world where she always had to be perfect for the camera for her to appreciate the laid-back comfortability of a small town in the heart of West Virginia's coal country.

"Are you sure you're up to it, Mama?"

Charlotte smiled. "Of course I'm sure. I don't need you working yourself down to the bone where you won't have enough strength to bake or even run a business. You've just begun putting on weight and I don't want folks saying that my baby girl looks like a scarecrow."

Sasha rolled her eyes upward. "Thanks, Mama." Pushing back her chair, she stood up. "I think I'm going to take a shower, because once I get into the tub, I won't be able to get out."

"Do you want me to come up and check on you?"

"Nah. I'm good." Rounding the table, she leaned down and kissed Charlotte's cheek. "Thank you for dinner. It was delicious."

"I'm going to put some away for tomorrow's lunch."

Turning on her heel, Sasha walked out of the kitchen, through the dining room and up the staircase to the second story. Charlotte had become a lifesaver and her lifeline. She had become her unofficial sous chef; she brought her lunch so she wouldn't have to leave the shop for a meal; and she'd been there for her to greet town officials and the walk-ins.

Sasha didn't know what she would've done if she hadn't had her mother. She entered her bedroom, stripped off her clothes and walked naked into the bathroom across the hall. She managed to brush her teeth and shower in under fifteen minutes. Within seconds of her head touching the pillow, she closed her eyes and fell asleep.

Chapter Three

Sasha woke early and was in the shop before five. She'd put up enough dough for marble rye, multigrain and several loaves of *pain de campagne*—a French country-style bread with a sourdough starter. She had also sent an email to the local church's outreach director that she had planned to donate any leftover baked goods for their soup-kitchen lunch program. There were several families in towns that had fallen on hard times and had to depend on the generosity of others to keep from going hungry.

Charlotte arrived twenty minutes before seven and checked the contents of the refrigerator showcase. She walked to the entrance of the kitchen. "Is the day's special ready for me to put in the showcase?"

Sasha's head popped up. "They're cooling now." She knew the red velvet cheesecake brownies would become a customer favorite because of the popularity of red velvet cake and brownies. And she hoped pairing them with cheesecake would take anyone that ate it by complete surprise.

She glanced up at the wall clock and realized she had less than forty minutes to make a dozen blueberry and oatmeal raisin muffins. It took muffins about fifteen to twenty minutes to bake and about five to cool. Sasha wanted to wait until she was certain she would have steady customers before she advertised for an assistant to help her in the kitchen. Creating specialty cakes required only one person, but it was not the same when she wanted to bake breads, pies and tortes. Sasha carefully placed slices of the cheesecake into a box and set it on a shelf in the refrigerator for Kiera, before putting the rest on a large baking sheet covered with paper doilies. She had cut small pieces as samples before she slid the sheet into the showcase.

Charlotte clasped her hands together. "That looks delicious."

Reaching for a toothpick, Sasha speared a sample and handed it to her mother. "Tell me what you think."

Shaking her head, while chewing and rolling her eyes upward, Charlotte moaned in satisfaction. "That's incredible. The raspberry drizzle really offsets the sourness of the cream cheese. This is a real winner. And I'm willing to bet folks will ask for it again and again."

"That's what I'm hoping."

"It's almost seven, so do you want me to raise the shades?" Charlotte asked.

"Yes. I'm going to bring out the muffins." While her mother manned the front, Sasha planned to bake small batches of Madeleine cookies, snickerdoodles, ginger, chocolate chip, sugar and cinnamon hazelnut biscotti. If or when they sold out, then she would know whether to increase the quantity or eliminate them from her list.

The morning passed quickly, and the chiming of the bell indicated a steady stream of customers. A few times Sasha had to come from the kitchen to assist Charlotte. She wore disposable clear plastic gloves when selecting the baked goods, and then removed them when handling money or credit cards. The transfer was rote for Charlotte, who'd spent thirty years working in food service. They both wore bouffant caps to prevent hair falling into the food.

Kiera arrived fifteen minutes early. Punctuality was a good sign for Sasha that she could depend on Kiera. "Come with me in the back and I'll show you where you can put your things." Kiera followed her to the kitchen, where she hung up her jacket. Sasha pointed to the teenage girl's three-inch booties. "Do you think you'll be able to stand comfortably in those, because you're going to be on your feet the whole time."

Kiera looked down at her shoes. "I can walk around in these all day."

Sasha wanted to tell her there were times during her school day when she was seated but decided to hold her tongue. And it was apparent Kiera was very confident with the heels that put her close to the five-ten mark. Sasha was five-nine in bare feet, and whenever she wore a pair of four-inch stilettos she towered over her ex— which was a bone of contention between them when she refused to attend a formal affair in ballet-type flats.

Sasha pointed to one of the three sinks she'd had the contractor install. "You can wash your hands over there. I'm going to give you something to cover your hair because we don't want our customers complaining of finding hair in their food. After that my mother will show you what to do."

She discovered Kiera was a quick study. Charlotte had stayed an extra hour to show the teenager how to man the front of the shop, and by the five o'clock hour Sasha had joined her taking and ringing up orders.

Kiera's dark eyes sparkled with excitement. "I can't believe you almost sold out everything."

"It was a good day," Sasha said in agreement. And that meant she had to come in even earlier the following morning.

"What do you plan to make tomorrow?"

"Cupcakes and mini pies."

"What about bread?" Kiera asked. "Because there's none left."

"I plan to always have fresh bread." And she knew she had to increase the quantity because she wanted to donate it to the church's soup kitchen. "It's time for you to leave. How are you getting home?"

"Daddy's going to pick me up. He doesn't see patients on Wednesdays."

Sasha nodded and remembered Dwight talked about Wednesday being golf day for doctors. "Why don't you go into the back and get your things? And don't forget to take the box with your name on it from the fridge."

The words were barely off her tongue when Dwight walked in. Her heart rate kicked into a higher gear as she stared at him. Today he was casually dressed in a pair of jeans, a gray sweatshirt stamped with the US Army insignia and Dr. Martens. He'd covered his head with a well-worn black baseball cap.

There was something intangible about the single dad

that pulled her in and refused to let her go when it hadn't been that way with other men, and that included Grant. Her ex had worked overtime to get her to go out with him, and at the time it fed her ego to have a man chase her. Dwight wasn't chasing her, didn't even appear to be interested in her, so she couldn't understand her reaction to him.

"How was her first day?" Dwight asked.

Resting her arms on the top of the showcase, Sasha smiled. "She's a pro."

"So, you're going to keep her?" he teased.

"I'll fight anyone trying to lure her away."

Throwing back his head, Dwight laughed. "That's serious."

"She's in the back getting her things." Sasha sobered. "You're very lucky, Dwight. Your daughter is a natural when it comes to interacting with the public."

"I must admit she had some experience last summer when she filled in for my receptionist."

"Do you expect her to work for you this summer?" Sasha was hard-pressed to keep the panic out of her voice.

Dwight shook his head. "No. If anything unforeseen comes up and my mother isn't busy, then she'll fill in."

Sasha rested a hand on her chest over her tunic. "Thank you."

Dwight gave Sasha a lingering stare, wondering what was different about her other than the hair bonnet. Suddenly it dawned on him that she wasn't wearing any makeup, unlike the day before, which had artfully concealed a sprinkling of freckles over her nose and cheeks. Her fresh-scrubbed face made her appear natural and wholesome.

Kiera emerged from the back of the shop, smiling and holding a red-and-white-striped box stamped with the shop's logo. "Daddy, I'm glad Miss Sasha saved some red velvet cheesecake brownies for us, because they were all sold out."

Dwight inclined his head. "I thank you, Miss Sasha, for you being generous *and* thoughtful."

Sasha, blushing, waved a hand. "There's no need to thank me. I should be the one thanking you for allowing Kiera to work here."

He noticed Kiera lowering her eyes, and it was apparent Sasha had embarrassed her. Even though he hadn't spent as much time with his daughter as he'd wanted, Dwight had come to recognize a certain shyness in her. He'd noticed boys her age staring at her while she pretended not to notice them. Maybe he was biased but there was no doubt she would become a beautiful woman like her mother. And it had been Adrienne's beauty and outgoing personality he hadn't been able to resist. They'd begun dating in high school and married within days of their respective college graduations.

"Daddy, I need to get home and do homework," Kiera said softly. Her head popped up. "I'll see you tomorrow, Miss Sasha. And thank you for the brownies."

"Tomorrow it is."

Dwight winked at Sasha and dropped his arm over Kiera's shoulders. He'd picked her up from school after her last class and drove her downtown. His mother had prepared a lunch for her granddaughter to eat before she began working. Victoria Adams had declared there was no way she was going to permit her grandbaby girl to miss a meal because of a job. She'd promised to pick her up from school on the days Dwight couldn't.

He knew his mother was overjoyed having her grand-daughter close to her every day instead of a month during the summer, and occasionally when she'd accompanied him during his trips to New York. Dwight was more than aware that his mother had never approved of his marrying Adrienne, and although her daughter-in-law had made her a grandmother, even today Victoria's impression of Kiera's mother hadn't changed.

Dwight pressed the remote device to the Jeep and opened the passenger-side door for Kiera. He rounded the vehicle and slipped behind the wheel. "How was your first day?"

Kiera ran a hand over her braided hair. "It was good except my feet hurt from standing up so much."

He glanced down at her shoes. He could not understand why his daughter insisted on wearing high heels, and when he'd questioned her, she claimed she liked standing out from among the shorter girls who'd treated her as if she was carrying a communicable disease.

That was the first time Dwight realized his daughter was regarded as an outsider in a school system where most of the kids had grown up together. Not only had Kiera acquired the sophistication of someone who'd grown up in a cosmopolitan city like New York City, but she'd also favored the ubiquitous black worn by many New Yorkers. She must have confided this to her grandmother when Dwight overheard his mother telling Kiera, "Don't concern yourself about those jealous little snits, because they know you're better born and better raised."

He had his mother to thank for telling Kiera what was so obvious, because it would not have come out like that if he'd had to say it. There were a few occasions when he'd waited to pick Kiera up from school and he'd noticed several boys staring at her. This had obviously annoyed some of the girls with them, and when he'd mentioned this to Kiera, she stated the girls did not have to worry about her coming on to their boyfriends because all of them were stupid. Dwight agreed that some teenage boys were stupid, but there would come a time when they became mature young men. However, his daughter was having none of his talk about boys and so he dropped the subject.

"Maybe you should bring a pair of tennis shoes with you that you can change into before you start working."

Kiera nodded. "I'm definitely going to do that."

Dwight drove out of the parking lot and came to a complete stop at the railroad crossing as the gates came down. The sound of ringing bells and flashing red lights indicated an oncoming train. "How was school today?"

Kiera shifted on her seat. "Daddy, remember you asked me that when you picked me up?"

He smiled. "My bad. I forgot about that. Your old man must be getting senile."

"You're not old and you're a long way from being senile. Maybe you need to take up a hobby."

"I have a hobby."

"What's that?"

"You, baby girl, and fishing." He'd become quite an adept at fly-fishing.

Kiera laughed. "I can't be your hobby." She sobered. "Have you thought about getting a girlfriend? Mom's married, so what's stopping you from marrying again?"

A frown found its way over Dwight's features. "I

don't have time for a girlfriend. Maybe after you go off to college I'll consider dating again."

"But that's not for more than a year, and you'll be too old to hit the clubs looking for a girlfriend."

His frown grew deeper. "What do you know about trolling clubs looking for dates?"

"I heard Mom say that you look for women in clubs."

Dwight felt a surge of rage he found hard to control and counted slowly until he once again felt in control. Adrienne had a tongue that was lethal as cyanide and sharp as a samurai sword. He had dated a few women since his divorce, and fortunately, he hadn't had to resort to going to clubs to pick them up.

He chose his words carefully, because the last thing Dwight wanted was to belittle Kiera's mother. It was enough that she didn't get along with her stepfather. "Your mother is wrong."

"Then why would she say that, Daddy?"

He forced a smile. "I don't know."

Kiera met his eyes. "Don't you want a girlfriend?"

Kiera was asking him questions he'd asked himself over and over since his divorce, and he knew if he hadn't a daughter he would've considered marrying again. There was one woman who lived in the state's capital that he'd dated off and on for nearly a year. She'd accused him of talking incessantly about his daughter and decided to end their liaison because she wasn't able to compete with her for his attention. One thing Dwight had promised himself was that he wasn't going to hide the fact that he was a single father and his daughter came first in his life.

"It's not that I don't want a girlfriend. It's just that I haven't met someone I want to spend time with."

"Does she have to be pretty?"

Dwight shook his head. "No, Kiera, looks are nice, but they're not everything. I'd like her to be well-rounded so we could have intelligent conversations. And it would help if we both like the same things."

"Are you saying she would have to be a dentist, too?"

"Oh, no," he drawled. "That definitely would be a deal breaker. I don't want someone where we'd spend all of our time talking about deciduous, cementum and molars." The last car on the train passed and the gates lifted, and Dwight drove over the tracks.

"What made you fall in love with Mom and marry her?"

Frowning through the windshield, he held the wheel in a death-like grip. "What's with the twenty questions, Kiera? Have you been talking to your mother and she's been interrogating you about me?"

Kiera stared straight ahead. She was so still she could've been carved out of stone. "The last time I spoke to her she did ask me if you had a girlfriend."

A muscle twitched in Dwight's jaw as he clenched his teeth. "The next time you talk to your mother and she asks about me, I want you to say, 'No comment.'"

"You know how Mom is. Grammie says she's like a dog with a bone."

"Well, this big dog isn't having it. I meant what I said about feeding her information about me."

He wanted to tell Kiera that if her mother was so interested in his love life, then she should've never divorced him. After all, she had moved on with a new husband in a new city and loved her work, and from what he could see, she was having the time of her life.

"I know she's going to get mad at me if I say that to her."

"Let me handle your mother, Kiera. We're both adults and I can say things to her you can't or shouldn't. Your mother legally handed over custody of you to me, so that means I'm totally responsible for you until you're twenty-one."

Kiera rested her left hand over his right on the steering wheel. "I'm glad I'm living with you. Thank you, Daddy."

He smiled. "You're welcome, sweetie."

He would never forget the sound of his daughter's sobbing when she called to tell him her mother had made plans to send her to a Connecticut boarding school because Kiera had talked back to her stepfather. The tables were reversed because Adrienne's husband had issued his own ultimatum: him or his stepdaughter.

Dwight had canceled all his appointments and flew up to New York with the intent of causing bodily harm to the man who'd promised him he would always protect Kiera. By the time the jet landed at LaGuardia Airport his temper had cooled considerably, and he was able to sit down and convince Adrienne their daughter would do well living with him.

It was his ex-wife's husband who convinced her to agree to Dwight's decision. Initially, Adrienne had balked because it meant losing child support, despite her earning a six-figure salary, but in the end after meeting with her lawyer, she signed the papers.

"I love you, Daddy."

Dwight smiled. "Love you more."

And he did. He could not imagine loving Kiera any more than he did. Although he and Adrienne had taken precautions to prevent an unplanned pregnancy, he never regretted becoming a father. He'd loved her just that much. However, it wasn't the same with Adrienne. Motherhood changed her into a sullen woman who resented having to stay home with a baby while he attended dental school. Dwight had promised his wife that as soon as he passed the dental boards and set up a practice, she could return to grad school to get her MBA.

No one was more shocked than Dwight when she filed for divorce because she didn't want to be the wife of a small-town dentist. He'd told her repeatedly that he didn't want to or could not afford to set up a practice in New York City. Blinded by the bright lights and mesmerized by the hustle and bustle of the Big Apple, where she'd attended college, Adrienne couldn't get it out of her system.

He drove into the driveway of his house, tapping the remote device on the visor to open the garage door. Kiera kicked off her booties and unbuckled her seat belt. She was out of the Jeep before Dwight shut off the engine. Shoes in hand, she walked gingerly up the stairs and opened the door that led directly into the mudroom. He followed, removing his boots and leaving them on a mat next to a slop sink.

"What's up with her?" Victoria Adams asked Dwight when he entered the kitchen.

"Her dogs are barking."

Victoria slowly shook her head. "I told that girl that she can't look cute standing around for hours in those heels."

He tried not to smile. "Hard head makes for a soft behind."

"Either it's a soft behind or bloody toes," Victoria drawled. She lifted the lid on a pot of rice. "I can remember the days when I used to go to dances in spikes and thought I was really cute until I had to walk home with my shoes in my hands."

Dwight handed his mother the box from Sasha's Sweet Shoppe. "You're still cute, Mom." He had always believed his mother was one of the most beautiful women in Wickham Falls. Tall, slender, with delicate features in a flawless sable complexion, she had been voted the prettiest girl in her graduating class. The once curly hair falling to her shoulders reminiscent of clusters of black grapes was now snow-white and styled in a pixie cut that hugged her head like a cap. "You don't have to make dessert because Sasha has promised to give Kiera whatever she offers as the day's special." He handed her the box with the cheesecake.

Victoria's large dark eyes, eyes Dwight had inherited, were bright with merriment. "Well, bless her heart. That's so nice of her. I need to stop in and buy something. The last time I was downtown she still wasn't open for business."

"Maybe you could get the ladies at the auxiliary to order dessert from her. After all, we need to do our part to support our local businesses."

"I'll definitely suggest it." She glanced at the clock on the microwave. "It's going to be another thirty or forty minutes before I finish dinner."

Dwight dropped a kiss on his mother's hair. "Do you need help with anything?"

"No, I'm good here."

"Are you sure?"

"Of course I'm sure, Dwight. Go and hang out in the family room until I call you."

Even though his mother had her own kitchen in the guesthouse, she preferred using his. He didn't complain because it reminded him of the times when he'd come home from school as a young boy to find his mother puttering around in the kitchen while preparing the evening meal. As an OR nurse, she had worked the 7:00 a.m. to 2:00 p.m. shift. Her shift never changed because she had to be home in time for her son at the end of the school day. His mother dropped him off at his paternal grandmother's house the night before and picked him up there when the bus dropped him off at the end of the day.

He rarely saw his special-agent father when he was assigned to the FBI's Behavioral Analysis Unit in Norfolk, Virginia. After a decade, Mathias requested a transfer and was approved to work closer to home for the Bureau's Criminal Justice Information Services in Clarksburg, West Virginia. Although he'd traded fieldwork for a desk assignment, the two-hour drive between Clarksburg and Wickham Falls was worth the sacrifice if only to see his wife and only child more often. Mathias's dream of retiring and taking his wife on an around-the-world cruise vanished when the car he was driving was hit when the driver of a tractor trailer fell asleep behind the wheel. He'd died instantly, and even after twelve years Victoria continued to mourn his passing.

Dwight had just folded his body down to his favorite chaise when he heard Kiera screaming, "Daddy, I can't find my cell phone!" He didn't bother to move because Kiera misplacing her phone had become a regular occurrence.

"Where was the last time you saw it?" he asked when she raced into the room.

"I know I had it when you picked me up from school, but…" Her words trailed off. "I must have left it at Miss Sasha's."

"Are you sure?"

An expression of uncertainty flittered over Kiera's face. "It's not in my backpack, so I had to put it in my jacket pocket."

"Check your pockets again."

"I did, Daddy, and it's not there."

"You know what this means if you can't find it." Kiera closed her eyes and bit her lip. Dwight knew she was trying not to cry. "Why don't you call Miss Sasha and ask her if you left it there?"

Kiera held out her hand, and rising slightly, Dwight gave her the cell phone he'd set on a side table. He waited, watching her expression brighten when she spoke quietly into the phone. "Thank you."

"What's up?" Dwight asked when she returned his phone.

"She said she's talking to a client. As soon as she finishes, she's going to look for it. And if she finds it, she'll text you, and bring it over later because she's very busy right now."

He didn't want to tell Kiera that she just might be putting others out of their way because of her carelessness. But he knew she felt bad enough without him reminding her of how many phones she'd lost or misplaced over the years.

"I promise not to—"

Dwight held up a hand, stopping her entreaty. "Please, Kiera, don't say anything else. I'll cancel your account if Sasha doesn't find your phone, but it's going to be at least three months before you get another one."

"You can't do that, Daddy!"

"Did you forget what you agreed to when you lost the last one?"

"No, but…"

"But nothing, Kiera. You've had three cell phones in less than six months."

Kiera stomped her foot in frustration. "That's not fair!"

"Life is not fair, baby girl," Dwight countered. "Once you're old enough to have your own account, then I don't care how many cell phones you lose," he said as she turned and walked out of the room. Picking up the remote device resting on a side table, he clicked on the television, channel surfing until he found one of his favorite sports programs. The ringtone on his phone indicated he had a text message.

Sasha: Found the phone. Will bring it over after 9.

Dwight: I will come and pick it up.

Sasha: Don't bother. I'll drop it off. I'll get your address from Kiera's application. Later.

Dwight was really annoyed that Kiera had been less than responsible with her phone. She claimed she needed one to maintain contact with her mother and some of her former New York City classmates. But that was not going to happen if she continued to lose phones. And if she wanted to call her mother or friends, then she would have to use her grandmother's landline or the one at his office. His daughter had always had a penchant for losing things when she was younger: mittens, gloves, hats, scarves and now phones. He used to tease her that she would lose her head if it hadn't been attached to her body.

When she'd misplaced her last phone, they'd made a pact that she would have to wait at least three months before he bought her another one. Fortunately, Sasha found it, so this time Kiera managed to dodge a bullet.

It was close to ten when Dwight stood on the porch as he waited for Sasha's arrival. She had sent him another text saying she was on her way. Lightly falling rain had changed over to sleet once the temperature dropped fifteen degrees in two hours, and he'd turned up the thermostat and started a fire in the family room's fireplace to ward off the sudden chill.

He saw a sweep of headlights as her van maneuvered into the driveway. He came down off the porch to meet her when she alighted from her vehicle. She'd exchanged her tunic for a white T-shirt. The scent of her perfume wafted to his nostrils with her approach as she rubbed her bare arms. He couldn't believe she'd gone out without a coat. A rising breeze lifted the curls framing her round face.

He cupped her elbow. "Please come into the house, where it's warm."

"I had no idea it was this cold until I left my house."

He opened the front door, standing off to the side to let her precede him. "You should always leave a jacket in your car."

Sasha turned her head so Dwight wouldn't see her gaping as she walked into his house. The two-story farmhouse with a wraparound porch was filled with furnishings for maximum comfort and practicality. She thought of the style as casual country that made her feel immediately at home with a desire to stay and put her feet up. The open floor plan with a great room and a combination of the kitchen, living, dining and family rooms allowed light and air to flow unchecked.

Warmth and the smell of burning wood enveloped her like a thick blanket. "It's nice and toasty in here."

"What if I make you a hot chocolate to warm you up?"

Sasha turned to find Dwight standing several feet away, hands clasped behind his back. Her intention was to come and drop off Kiera's cell phone and then leave, but now she wasn't so certain she wanted to go back home. "I'd like that, thank you." Reaching into the pocket of her jeans, she handed him the phone. "She left it on a chair."

Dwight set it on the glass-topped coffee table. "Do you take your chocolate with whipped cream?"

Sasha smiled. "But of course."

He reached for her hand and led her into the family room. "Sit and warm up. I'll be right back."

She sat on a cream-covered upholstered armchair stamped with jade green leaves. Kicking off her flip-flops, she rested her bare feet on the matching footstool. Sasha did not know what had possessed her to leave the house in mid-February wearing only a T-shirt, jeans and summer footwear. Pressing her head against the back of the chair, she closed her eyes. She'd prided herself on being levelheaded, rational and always assessing a situation before acting. But somehow all was forgotten whenever she and Dwight Adams occupied the same space. Sasha did not know what it was about the man that had her reacting to him like a starstruck adolescent.

When he'd offered to come over to pick up his daughter's phone, Sasha had refused because curiosity overrode what was easier. He'd been divorced for more than a decade and she wanted to know if his home reflected his life as a bachelor father. However, his furnishings suggested a preference for a home filled with the interaction of family and friends.

Shifting on the chair, she studied a group of photographs on a side table. There was one of Dwight's parents in their college graduation finery and another of Dwight in his dress army uniform. The oak leaves on his collar identified him as a major. She smiled when staring at a photo of a younger grinning Dwight holding Kiera, who'd pressed her mouth against her father's cheek.

Her gaze shifted as she stared at the flickering flames behind the decorative fireplace screen. Nowhere in any of the photos had there been an image of Kiera's mother, and she wondered if Dwight's ex-wife had been responsible for decorating the house, and if he'd elected not to change it because it was a constant reminder of the woman he'd loved and married. Her musings about the man were interrupted when he returned and handed her a mug of steaming chocolate topped with a froth of whipped cream.

Sitting straight, she took the mug, her fingers brushing against his before he took a facing chair. "Thank you. Aren't you going to have some?" she asked.

Dwight stared at her under lowered lids. "No. I had a cup of coffee just before you got here."

Sasha tightened her hold on the hot mug. "Your home is beautiful."

He inclined his head. "Thank you."

She took a sip and the warmth in her throat and chest had nothing to do with the heated liquid, but with the way Dwight was looking at her. Why again, she thought, did she feel like a specimen under a microscope?

"Was this the original design when you moved in?" Sasha asked. She had to talk, do something other than stare at Dwight staring back at her. "I have never been in any of the homes on this side of town," she explained. Wickham Falls had a population under five thousand, yet the social lines were as clearly drawn as borders separating one state from another.

Stretching out his legs, Dwight crossed his feet at the ankles. "I had a contractor remove the walls after my divorce."

Dwight mentioning the divorce gave Sasha the opening she needed to delve into his personal life. "Do you miss being married?"

Inky-black eyebrows rose slightly with her question. "No. In fact, I like being single. But how about you, Sasha?"

"What about me, Dwight?"

"How difficult was it for you to give up your celebrity lifestyle and marriage to one of the biggest country recording stars on the planet to come back to a place with two stoplights and railroad tracks running through the middle of the downtown business district?"

Chapter Four

Sasha stared at the rapidly fading whipped cream before she looked directly at Dwight. "It was the easiest decision I'd ever had to make in my life."

"So, you don't regret coming back?"

"Not in the least." She took another sip of the semisweet liquid and then set the mug on a glass coaster on the table. She stood up. "It's getting late and I've taken up enough of your time."

Sasha did not want to tell Dwight that she wasn't ready to bare her soul about the details of her failed marriage. She did not know why it mattered, but she didn't want him to think of her as a small-town girl who'd allowed herself to get bedazzled and sucked in by the hype and glamour of America's Music City, where she'd married Nashville's hottest singing sensation after a three-month whirlwind romance.

Dwight also stood. "Don't leave yet. I want to get something for you." He walked out of the family room and returned minutes later with a military fatigue jacket and a small folding umbrella. "Please put on the jacket. We can't have you getting sick and having to close down so soon after your grand opening."

Sasha held out her arms as he helped her into it. The lingering scent of his cologne clung to the fabric. She wondered if his concern was because he was a doctor or a father. "I'll give it back when I see you again."

"You can keep it. I happen to have a few of them."

"If that's the case, then I'm going to leave it in the van in case I again decide to challenge Mother Nature."

"And don't forget a pair of shoes," Dwight teased with a wide grin.

She wiggled her bare toes painted a vermilion red. "I must be a country girl down to the marrow in my bones, because I love going barefoot."

Dwight slowly shook his head as he handed her the umbrella. "Even country girls know to wear shoes in the winter."

Going on tiptoe, Sasha kissed his cheek. "I really appreciate your concern."

Turning on her heel, she made her way to the front door, waiting for him to open it. She opened the umbrella, raced down the porch steps and over to her vehicle. A light layer of ice had covered the windshield. Touching the handle on the driver's-side door, she unlocked it and slipped in. As she tapped the start button, the engine roared to life. She closed the umbrella, leaving it on the mat behind the seat, and then turned the heat to the highest setting. She peered through the side window to find Dwight standing under the protection of the porch, watching her. It took several minutes to defrost the windshield before she fastened her seat belt and backed out of the driveway.

It wasn't until she turned off onto the road leading to her house that she chided herself for kissing Dwight. It hadn't mattered that it was a chaste one; she still shouldn't have done it.

"I'm losing it," she whispered to herself.

There was no doubt she wouldn't have had any interaction with the man if his daughter hadn't come to apply to work in the bakeshop. The only other alternative would have been if she became one of his patients. She had another month before her semiannual checkup and she planned to call the dental office in Mineral Springs, where she'd gone as a child, for an appointment.

Sasha continued to ask herself what it was about Dwight Adams that made her heart beat a little too fast to make her feel completely at ease around him. It hadn't been that way in the past when he'd come to her house to pick up her brother, because she knew he had a steady girlfriend. Even if he hadn't been dating Adrienne, she doubted whether Dwight would have asked her out because of their six-year age difference. That was then, but this was now. And it wasn't that there weren't mixed-race couples in Wickham Falls, and if she did date Dwight, they wouldn't turn heads if seen together. If folks did whisper, it would be about her capturing the attention of one of The Falls' most eligible bachelors. She didn't want to overthink or indulge in what she deemed fantasy, because there was no guarantee anything would come from her association with her employee's father other than friendship.

She made it home, unlocked the door and tiptoed

up the staircase to her bedroom so as not to disturb her mother. Sasha left Dwight's jacket on the back of a chair, slipped out of her clothes and pulled a night-gown over her head. After brushing her teeth, she set her alarm for five, got into bed and pulled the blankets up and over her shoulders. The incessant tapping of sleet against the windows was the perfect antidote to lull her to sleep. Morpheus claimed her, as she shut out the image of Dwight's dimpled smile and penetrating dark eyes that appeared to look not at her but through her to know what she was thinking, and that she liked him the way a woman liked a man.

Leaning over his reclining patient, Dwight used a light touch as he drilled a young boy's tooth. The four-year-old appeared totally oblivious to the sound of the drill as he concentrated on the images on the virtual-reality headset. Although his shingle advertised family dentistry, he counted more children than adults among his patients, which had earned him the reputation as the most popular pediatric dentist in the county. Children looked forward to sitting in his chairs. Video games and headsets were the perfect solution to distract kids if they required a local anesthesia, while a trio of wall-mounted televisions in the waiting room tuned to cooking, car-toon and all-news stations kept most of his patients oc-cupied while they waited to be seen.

He removed the decay and then placed a sealer on the tooth prior to filling it with a tooth-colored com-posite resin to protect the tooth and minimize sensitiv-ity. Rather than traumatize the boy with an injection of procaine, he'd applied a numbing gel to his gum, lip and cheek. Dwight checked to make sure the boy's bite was okay and adjusted the filling. He took off the latex gloves, discarding them in a designated container, and nodded to the assistant to finish up with the patient.

Dwight found it disturbing to treat a patient as young as four with cavities in his primary teeth. It indicated either poor dental hygiene or a diet of sugary foods in which plaque built up on the tooth and caused decay. Although he'd spoken at length to the child's mother about brushing his teeth after each meal and limiting his intake of candy and pop, it was obvious his advice and recommendations had fallen on deaf ears. This was the third tooth he'd filled for the child. His practice's motto was: Good Dental Health Is A Family Affair, and fortunately, most of his patients had embraced it.

He returned to his office and discovered the blinking red light on his private line. Tapping the button, he listened to his mother's voice-mail message. It was a rare occasion that Victoria called him at his office.

Picking up his cell phone, he scrolled through the directory until he found her number. "Yes, Mom."

"Are you still going to your lake house this weekend?"

"I've been thinking about it. Why?" Dwight had purchased the cabin in the gated community touted as a fisherman's nirvana. All the modern cabins claimed central air and heating and had direct paths that led to the lake. It was where he'd spent most of his weekends relaxing, fishing and occasionally socializing with a few retirees who lived there year-round. The weeks had passed quickly, and it was now late March, and spring had come to West Virginia with warmer temperatures and a profusion of flowers, lush lawns and verdant valleys.

"Kiera invited Sasha and her mother over for Sunday dinner."

Dwight sat straight. He'd asked Kiera if she wanted to go with him to the lake and she'd said she would have to think about it. Well, it was apparent her thinking about it meant she'd had other intentions.

"What did you say?"

"I told her I'm open to it, only because she can't stop talking about how much she likes Sasha and Charlotte, and also loves working in their shop."

Dwight focused on the framed diplomas, degrees and licenses on the opposite wall. He had made the decision, following the night Sasha came to his house to return Kiera's cell phone, to limit his contact with her. There was something about the redhead that stirred feelings he did not want to feel, and he knew becoming involved with his daughter's employer would not be to their advantage. Not only did they live in the same town, but they were also highly visible as downtown business owners.

What he could not deny was his attraction to the bubbly pastry chef. He liked her smile, infectious laugh and her generosity. There were times when she exhibited a modicum of shyness and vulnerability that appealed to his protective nature. However, it was never far from his mind that Sasha had earned a reputation as a celebrity chef who had become the wife of Nashville royalty.

What he did not understand was why she had given it all up to come back to a town that barely made the map. A town whose history was filled with generations that had worked in the coal mines under the control of unscrupulous owners that preferred closing the mines to installing government-mandated safety equipment, leaving workers without an alternative source of income.

In later years, career day at the high school was a boon for recruiters from every branch of the armed forces who enticed graduating seniors with offers of signing bonuses to join the military. Dwight graduated Texas A&M, attended dental school and then set up his practice in The Falls while serving in the army reserves as a dental corps officer. As a US Medical Department officer and as a reservist, he was required to attend the Ordnance Basic Officer Leader Course for two weeks rather than the ten to fourteen weeks for active duty officers. He'd been fortunate enough to combine his passions for the military and dentistry, but recently had to sacrifice the former to become a full-time dad.

"What do you want me to say, Mom? Uninvite them?"

"No, Dwight. I expect you to say yes. After all, we'll be eating at your house."

Dwight shook his head. "What's wrong with your house?"

"Nothing, except that I like cooking in your kitchen."

Dwight did not want to believe what he was hearing. Although the kitchen in the guesthouse was smaller than his, Victoria had insisted it be equipped with top-of-the-line appliances. "If that's the case, why don't you consider moving in with me?"

"I told you before, I like living by myself because I don't need my son monitoring my whereabouts."

"It wouldn't bother me if you got a boyfriend," he teased.

"Bite your tongue, Dwight Mathias Adams. I was married too long, and more importantly, I don't have the patience to put up with another man. You're the one that should be dating. After all, you're not getting any younger."

Dwight sobered. "I told you before that I can't afford to get serious about anyone until Kiera goes off to college."

"I hope you're not suggesting you need her permission to take up with a woman."

"Of course not, Mom. Right now, she needs to know she has a full-time father, and not some man who has been in and out of her life for the past sixteen years."

"You really don't give your daughter enough credit," Victoria said. "She knows you love her and that you would do anything for her, but I'm willing to bet that she doesn't want you to sacrifice having a relationship with a woman because of your obligation as her father."

A beat passed, before Dwight said, "It sounds as if you two have been discussing my love life."

"Correction, son. Lack of love life."

He had to agree with his mother, but he wasn't about to admit that to her. "I don't have a problem with Sasha and her mother coming for dinner," he said instead.

"Good. I'll tell Kiera to let them know we'll be expecting them."

Dwight ended the call somehow feeling he'd been set up by his mother and daughter as they attempted to play matchmaker. He then wondered if Sasha had intimated to Kiera that she was interested in her father. When he recalled their few encounters there was nothing in her actions that indicated that she wanted anything beyond being acquaintances. He was Kiera's father and Sasha Kiera's employer, and that was where their association began and ended.

* * *

Sasha bit back a smile when she heard Charlotte's intake of breath as she drove her mother's car into the driveway leading to Dwight's home. It had been more than a month since their last encounter, and Sasha wondered if she'd crossed the line when she'd kissed him. He hadn't been repulsed or appeared shocked by the gesture, but that did not stop her from mentally beating up on herself for initiating it. After all, she did not know whether he was involved with or committed to another woman, which could have explained his keeping his distance. She finally had to remind herself that she was a thirty-two-year-old divorcée with a business to run, and that had to be her sole focus.

"The doctor has a very nice house," Charlotte whispered softly.

"Yes, he does," Sasha agreed. Navy blue siding, white trim and blue-and-white wicker porch furniture made the structure a standout among those on the block. The United States and Go Army flags suspended on a flagpole fluttered in the warm air. It had become a tradition for those serving or who had served in the military to fly flags and pennants representing their branches to proudly display them on lawns or porch posts.

Charlotte made a guttural sound, as if clearing her throat. "I don't understand what would make a woman walk away from all of this to live in a city with folks falling over one another just to exist."

Sasha came to a complete stop and shut off the engine. "Different strokes for different folks."

Charlotte unbuckled her seat belt. "Like you, Natasha? Don't forget, there was a time when you couldn't wait to leave town."

She got out of the Corolla, opened the rear door and picked up the large shopping bag with boxes of tarts, tortes and an assortment of mini cakes and pies. It was apparent Charlotte had forgotten and Sasha did not want to remind her mother that the constant squabbling between her and her husband had forced their children to leave home as soon as they'd graduated high school.

Sasha waited for Charlotte to alight from the car, and together they walked up to the porch. The front door opened, and she came face-to-face with Dwight for the first time in more than a month. An unconscious smile parted her lips as he stared at her as if she were a stranger. She knew he was taken aback by her metamorphosis. A sleek hairstyle, the black sheath dress, with an asymmetrical neckline, ending at her knees and a pair of matching kitten heels had replaced the tunic, loose-fitting pants and comfortable clogs she wore in the bakeshop. Sasha had also subtly made up her face to bring attention to her green eyes and mouth with a smoky-grayish eye shadow and a burnt-orange lip color. Taming her flyaway curls had proved challenging until she'd exchanged the blow-dryer for a flat iron. She'd rationalized that she was going to someone's house for Sunday dinner; therefore, she needed to step up her game.

Dwight smiled slowly as his gaze shifted from Sasha to Charlotte. He opened the door wider. "Welcome."

Sasha handed him the shopping bag. "I brought a little something for dessert."

Dwight peered into the bag. "It appears to be more than a little something."

"Grammie, they're here!" Kiera shouted as she raced

over to greet them. Sasha noticed the slight frown furrowing Dwight's forehead, but it disappeared quickly when Kiera clapped a hand over her mouth. "Sorry about yelling in the house, Daddy," she said, apologizing.

He handed Kiera the shopping bag. "Please take this into the kitchen." He returned his attention to his guests. "Please come in and sit down. My mother is just finishing up with everything."

Sasha followed him through the great room, noticing that the dining room table had been set with china, silver and crystal; a vase overflowing with an abundance of white roses and tulips served as the table's centerpiece.

Charlotte touched Sasha's arm. "I'm going to the kitchen to see if I can help Mrs. Adams."

"Do you think that's such a good idea?" Sasha whispered to Dwight as he cupped her elbow and led her over to a sand-colored sofa. "Cooks are usually very territorial when it comes to their kitchens." She sat, and he took the cushion next to her.

"It'll be all right. My mother doesn't want anyone to share her kitchen, but it's different with mine."

Sasha stared at him, seeing laughter in the dark eyes. "Your mother doesn't live with you?" She'd asked the question because Kiera would talk about her grandmother as if they all occupied the same house.

"My mother lives in a guesthouse at the back of this one. Once my father passed away, I'd invited her to live with me, but she claims she likes having her independence to come and go by her leave. So, when I suggested she sell the house where I'd grown up and let me build something practical for her on the half acre at the back of the house, she finally gave in. I must admit that it's quite nice. She has two bedrooms, a full bath, galley kitchen, and a living and dining area that over-looks the back deck. Last year she planted a flower and vegetable garden."

Sasha stared at the beige-and-teal woven area rug rather than the man sitting only inches away from her. The warmth of his body intensified the masculine scent of his cologne, which only served to trigger the erotic thoughts she had managed to repress during their sepa-ration. At that moment she had to question herself lust-ing after a man who didn't seem even remotely attracted to her, and knew it was hopeless to even conceive of a possible relationship with Dwight Adams.

"How's business?"

His deep sonorous voice had shattered her musings. "Didn't Kiera tell you?" she asked.

He shifted on the sofa, the motion bringing them even closer together. "Tell me what?"

"That your mother stopped in one day to order tea cakes for the Volunteer Fireman's Ladies Auxiliary. The women liked them so much that a number of them came into the shop during the week to place orders for other pastries."

"Word of mouth does go a long way in a small town," Dwight said. He paused. "Right now, I'm willing to bet that my mother is trying to get yours to join one of her civic organizations. Victoria Adams is one of the best when it comes to recruiting folks to join local clubs. She complains that most have the same members year after year, because many of them aren't willing to ac-cept new people with new ideas."

"It's called control, Dwight. They don't like relinquishing their power to others they may deem outsiders."

"Perhaps you're right."

"I know I am," Sasha countered quickly. She did not want to tell Dwight that most of the women that belonged to the civic and social organizations had a lot in common. Practically all were college educated, and their husbands were either businessmen or had attained some political standing in Wickham Falls.

"Hopefully my mother can convince yours to join the Ladies Auxiliary, because they'll be hosting a fundraiser in a couple of months to raise money for a new ambulance for first responders."

Sasha knew the group met at noon on Wednesdays, and if her mother did become a member, then she would have to man the front of the shop until Kiera arrived at one. The more she thought about it, the more she warmed to the possibility of Charlotte becoming involved with a local civic organization. It would give her mother something else to do other than work in the bakeshop.

"I think it would do Mama some good to get involved in things affecting The Falls." Secretly Sasha hoped Charlotte would meet a man who might respect her more than her late husband had.

"Now that you're a business owner, do you plan to join the chamber of commerce?"

Sasha nodded. "It's funny you ask, because one of the members came into the shop the other day and left an application and a ticket for their annual dinner dance. He did apologize for the short notice because the event is next weekend."

"Do you plan to attend?"

"No," Sasha replied. "I'll pay for the ticket and probably give it to one of my regular customers."

"You can give it away if you want, but I'd like you to go with me."

Sasha went completely still once she realized Dwight was asking her to be his date for a semiformal affair. "You have two tickets?"

He smiled, flashing dimples. "Yes. I always buy two because it's for a good cause."

She blinked slowly. "You don't have a date?"

"No. I usually take my mother, but this year she agreed to stay home with Kiera. She's trying to cut down on the number of social events she attends during the year. She has the Ladies Auxiliary and she's also involved in several military causes that include the Wounded Warrior Project."

"Don't you have someone else who can go with you?" Sasha knew she was asking a litany of questions, but she had to know if there was another woman in Dwight's life before agreeing to be his date for the night.

"No. That's why I'm asking you. But if you don't want to be seen with—"

"Don't say it," she said, cutting him off. "I'm truly honored that you asked me to be your date."

And she was honored. He was the first man she'd found herself liking enough to date since her divorce, and now that Dwight had asked her to go to the fundraiser with him, her fantasies were about to become a reality. There had been men who had come on to her before and after her marriage, but Sasha always felt that they had an ulterior motive. Before marrying Grant, she'd believed it was because they'd recognized her from the televised cooking competition, and once she was divorced it had been her high-profile marriage to a recording superstar.

But none of that appeared to faze Dwight. To him, she was a small-town girl who'd become a popular celebrity chef, but then left the bright lights to return home and to open a sweet shop. She had lost count of the number of folks who came into the bakeshop to either stare at her or ask about her failed marriage whenever she manned the front. It was as if they were more interested in her personal life than in making a purchase.

"Folks are really going to be shocked to see us attend together."

Dwight chuckled under his breath. "You're right about that." He paused. "What do you think about giving them a preview?"

Vertical lines appeared between Sasha's eyes. "A preview how?"

"Come with me tomorrow night to the Wolf Den for Military Monday. We can hang out for a couple of hours to give folks an opportunity to see us together. I can pick you up at seven and have you back home around nine, because I know you get up very early."

It was Sasha's turn to laugh. "I'm willing to bet gossip will spread throughout The Falls like a lighted fuse. If *The Sentinel* had a gossip column, we certainly would be included."

Dwight nodded, smiling. "And like the song, we'll give them something to talk about."

Sasha leaned to her right, their shoulders touching. "You're so bad," she teased.

"Guilty as charged, as long as it's a good bad."

For a reason she did not want to understand, Sasha was looking forward to being seen in public with Dwight

Adams. Aside from his good looks, she admired his unwavering devotion to Kiera. When living in Nashville, she'd met and socialized with divorced and single fathers whose priorities weren't their children but chasing the next woman. And based on their behavior, she had come to believe just paying child support was not the benchmark for being a good father. Her parents may have argued constantly as if their very existence depended upon it, but there was never a time when her father hadn't been there for his children.

"Isn't good bad an oxymoron?" she questioned.

"It all depends on the context."

Dwight covered Sasha's hand resting on the cushion with his. He threaded their fingers together. Her hand was cool, but not as cold as when she'd admitted to having cold hands and a warm heart. He knew he had taken a chance and risked being rejected but hoped beyond hope that she would agree to go to what had become the social event of the year. Everyone who owned a business in Wickham Falls would be there. And having her agree to go to the Den with him would be an extra bonus.

The fund-raiser gave folks a reason to dress up and let their hair down once dinner was over and dancing began. The local dry cleaner did a brisk business cleaning tuxedos and dress suits, while women made certain not to be seen in the same gown or dress they'd worn the year before. Dwight always enjoyed the gathering because residents were more than generous when it came to support of their local businesses.

He gave her fingers a gentle squeeze before releasing them and stood up. "Don't move. I'm needed to help carry the food to the table."

He walked past the dining room and into the kitchen and picked up a large platter with fried chicken. Victoria, after viewing an infomercial, had purchased an air fryer and sang its praises in her attempt to fry chicken without using oil. Not only was the method faster but also healthier than frying it on the stove. After that it had become her go-to appliance for cooking chicken and meat. Dwight set the platter on the dining room table. Kiera joined him as she filled goblets with sparkling water.

"I think Grammie cooked too much food," she said *sotto voce.*

"Not to worry, sweetie. None of it will go to waste because we'll be eating leftovers for the rest of the week."

"I heard that, Dwight," Victoria called out.

He gave Kiera a sidelong glance. "Your grandmother must have ears like a bat," he said between clenched teeth.

Kiera nodded. "I know, Daddy," she whispered.

Dwight returned to the kitchen and picked up two more platters, one with braised beef short ribs and the other with caramelized pork chops. Whenever Victoria volunteered to cook Sunday dinner it wasn't the ubiquitous Southern menu of fried chicken, sweet potatoes, collard greens, corn bread and pound cake or peach cobbler for dessert, but a variety of meats and sides that would become leftovers for lunch and dinner for several days.

Today she'd prepared her celebrated potato salad, sautéed carrots and garlicky spinach, and a field-green-and-apple salad. Victoria had taught Dwight to cook as soon as he was tall enough to look over the stove. She'd said she did not want her son to depend on a woman to feed him because he was unable to put together a palatable meal for himself. He opened a bottle of red wine and a rosé to allow them to breathe before filling the wineglasses. A carafe of sparkling lemonade was positioned at Kiera's place setting. Dwight seated his mother at the head of the table, and then Charlotte at the opposite end. He sat on his mother's right, while Kiera and Sasha sat together.

Victoria raised her water glass, everyone following suit. "Here's to friends and family. May this not be the last time we eat together."

"Are we going to do this every Sunday, Grammie?" Kiera asked.

"We certainly don't want to put your grandmother out every Sunday," Charlotte said before Victoria could answer her granddaughter. "I'd like to host next Sunday—that is, if you don't mind. It's been many years since I've cooked for more than one person. And that only changed recently since Natasha's come back."

Victoria looked directly at Dwight. "I can make it, but you'll have to ask Dwight about his intentions, because now that the weather has changed, he spends most weekends at his lake house."

"Daddy says once he gives up drilling teeth, he's going to become a professional fisherman."

"What happened to Dwight and Daddy speaking for himself?" Dwight questioned as he glared at Victoria and then Kiera.

Kiera ignored his slight reprimand when she said, "He's tried to teach me to fish, but the only thing I want to do with fish is eat it."

Sasha's pale eyebrows rose slightly. "What do you catch?"

Remnants of his annoyance with his mother and daughter lingered around the fringes of his mind when he shifted his attention to Sasha. "Rainbow trout and smallmouth bass."

"Do you clean and cook your catch?"

He nodded. "What I don't cook I clean and bring home and freeze."

"Daddy, can Miss Sasha come with us the next time we go to the lake house?"

Suddenly Dwight felt as if he was being put on the spot. First his mother had disclosed his future weekend plans and now his daughter was asking if he could include her employer. The few times Kiera had accompanied him, she complained about having nothing to do or no one to talk to. She didn't like getting up early to stand in water waiting to reel in fish, and she'd complained incessantly about cleaning their catch, but then said it was worth it when she sat down to eat grilled fish.

"That's something I'll have to discuss with Miss Sasha, because she just may have plans for her weekends." His explanation seemed to satisfy Kiera when she picked up the glass of lemonade and took a long swallow.

Dinner continued with Charlotte complimenting Victoria on her amazing buttermilk air-fried chicken, molasses-braised short ribs and potato salad. "I don't know whether I will be able to come close to matching this scrumptious feast."

"Mama's being modest, Miss Victoria. She's also a great cook."

Victoria winked at Sasha. "I'm sure she is."

Charlotte sat up straight. "Does this mean we're on for next Sunday?" Everyone sitting at the table nodded.

"What time should you expect us?" Dwight asked.

A network of faint lines fanned out around Charlotte's blue eyes when she smiled. "Four. Is that too late for you?"

"Not at all," he replied. "It's just that the chamber's dinner dance is the night before and I'll probably need time to recuperate from the festivities."

"Dwight and I are going together." Sasha's announcement appeared to stun everyone as a swollen silence ensued.

Dwight peered at her over the rim of his wineglass at the same time amusement shimmered in his dark eyes. Well, he thought, the cat was truly out of the bag. Sasha accompanying him as his date was certain to have tongues wagging. The only and last woman he'd dated from Wickham Falls he married. And he'd been forthcoming with Sasha when he told her he liked being single. But even more important, he had no intention of contemplating getting serious with a woman until his daughter left for college.

He also did not want a repeat of his last relationship, where he had been forced to choose between her or Kiera. It had been the second time in his adult life where a woman had issued an ultimatum. The first had been when his daughter's mother wanted him to choose between living in Wickham Falls and New York.

Victoria pushed back her chair and stood. "It's going to be a while before I bring out dessert and set up the

Viennese table, so I'm going to show Charlotte my place and the gardens." A slight blush suffused Sasha's face at the mention of the number of desserts.

Dwight also stood. "I'll clear the table and put away the leftovers."

Sasha rose to her feet. "I'll help you."

Kiera drained her glass of lemonade. "Daddy, can I go to Alexis's house to study for our chemistry test?"

"Okay. Just don't come back too late." She and the next-door neighbor's daughter had played with each other whenever Kiera had come to spend the summers with him Dwight waited until he was alone in the house with Sasha and said, "I do believe you shocked everyone when you mentioned going to the dinner dance with me."

Sasha clapped a hand over her mouth to smother her laughter. "Did you see my mother's face when I said it? I thought she was going to faint away."

Dwight smiled as he stacked dishes and serving pieces. "And I can't believe my mother did not have a comeback."

Carrying a platter of chicken, Sasha followed him into the kitchen. "Can you imagine what their reaction would be if we told them we were getting married?"

He went completely still and then set the dishes on the countertop. "No, I can't."

"Neither can I. The first time I married it was for all the wrong reasons, and I promised myself if or when I did marry again it would have to be because of love."

Dwight gave her an incredulous stare. "You weren't in love with your husband?"

"I tried to convince myself that I was, yet in the end, I knew I was deceiving him and myself."

"I know this is a very personal question, but did you marry him because he was a superstar recording artist?"

Chapter Five

Sasha's eyelids fluttered wildly. "No." Grant was not only charming, but he projected a larger-than-life persona she hadn't been able to resist.

"How long had you been dating?"

"A little less than three months. But even if I'd dated Grant for a year, I realized in the end that I wasn't cut out to be a celebrity wife."

"Maybe he couldn't accept that his wife was a celebrity in her own right."

Sasha's jaw dropped. She tried to speak but it was as if her voice locked in her throat. She did not want to believe she was that transparent, or maybe Dwight was just that perceptive. She nodded instead.

"Did he hurt you?"

"Not physically, but emotionally, where the scars weren't visible," she admitted as tears filled her eyes.

Taking a step, Dwight pulled her into an embrace, his chin resting on the top of her head. "It's okay, sweetie. He can't hurt you now."

Sasha buried her face against his shoulder and wrapped her arms around his waist. Feeling Dwight's warmth and strength, she felt safe, protected. The strong, steady pumping of his heart against her breasts had become a soothing salve as hers pounded a runaway rhythm. "My marriage was a mess."

Lowering his head, Dwight brushed a light kiss over her parted lips. "I don't want to ruin what has been a wonderful afternoon talking about *him* right about now."

Sasha knew he was right. The afternoon was as close to perfect as she could have wanted. His family had invited hers into their home, making her and her mother truly welcomed and a part of theirs. Dwight kissed her again, this time on the forehead.

Easing back, she smiled up at him, and she was rewarded with a dimpled smile in return from him. She dropped her arms, turned on her heel and returned to the dining room to gather more plates. Sasha had been ready to bare her soul to Dwight, to tell him things no other person knew other than her mother, if only to unburden herself. In the end, Charlotte had blamed herself because she hadn't set the best example for her daughter to follow. Both had married men who'd felt the need to control their wives.

Sasha and Dwight made quick work of clearing away the remains of dinner and storing leftovers in microwave glass containers with snap-lock lids. She'd just lined the buffet server with plates filled with an assortment of desserts when Charlotte and Victoria returned.

Forty-five minutes later, Sasha settled Charlotte in the Corolla, waiting until she secured her seat belt, and then rounded the compact car to sit beside her. They'd spent more than four hours with the Adamses and Sasha looked forward to going home and relaxing with the knowledge she would not have to get up early the following morning because the sweet shop was closed on Mondays.

"What did I miss while Victoria and I were gone?" Charlotte asked, as Sasha put the car in Reverse and backed out of the driveway.

"What are you talking about?"

"I asked Victoria if I could see her place to give you and Dwight some time alone."

Sasha's right foot hit the brake so hard the car lurched to a stop. "You did what?"

"There's no need to get your nose out of joint, Natasha. Even before you said you were going out with Dwight next weekend, I saw how he was staring at you when he opened the door. And anyone who isn't visually impaired could see what you've tried so hard to hide."

"And what's that, Mama?"

"That you like each other."

Easing off the brake, Sasha continued driving, her teeth clenched so tightly that her jaw ached. She'd wanted to scream at her mother, to remind her that she was an adult and did not need her as a go-between to help her attract a man. "I'm not going to lie and say I don't like Dwight, but you have no right to try to play matchmaker."

Charlotte stared out the side window. "I'm sorry. You can call me a meddling old fool if you want."

"Don't start with the guilt trip, Mama. I know you

want the best for me, but that's not going to happen until you let me experience life on my own, and to learn from my own mistakes and hopefully never repeat them."

"I know I never asked you, but do you want to get married again?"

Sasha pondered the question for several seconds. "If I found someone I loved and wanted to spend the rest of my life with—then yes."

Shifting slightly, Charlotte turned and looked at her. "You didn't see yourself when you came back to The Falls, Natasha. Not only did you look like the walking dead, but you were so angry that I was afraid to say anything to you. I know if I'd had a different temperament after you told me how Grant treated you, I would've driven to Nashville and—"

"Don't say it, Mama," Sasha said, cutting her off. "Grant is my past and you don't have to think or talk about what you'd liked or wanted to do to him."

"What I couldn't understand was why you didn't say something to me whenever we talked. If you'd given me the slightest hint of what you'd been going through with him, I would've told you to leave the son of a bitch."

"Mama! When did you start cussin'?"

Charlotte made a sucking sound with her tongue and teeth. "I did a lot of cussin' when your father was alive. It's just that I wouldn't let my kids hear it."

"So, you gave as good as you got?"

"Damn straight. Harold Manning knew I wouldn't cuss him out when our kids were around, so he knew when to start up with me."

"Why did you marry him, Mama?"

A beat passed. "Your father and I went out a few times, and the first time we slept together, he got me pregnant.

And when I told him, he insisted we get married. His folks never married, and that always bothered him. And if I hadn't married him, then you wouldn't be here. And that's something I've never regretted. I wanted and love all my children."

"Why didn't Grandma and Pops get married?"

"Your grandma's first husband refused to give her a divorce, so she left him and moved in with Pops. They had a bunch of kids and lived together as common-law husband and wife even if the state of West Virginia doesn't recognize it."

"The fact that you married Dad should've been enough for him."

"Harold was just an angry man, Natasha. After a while, I realized no one or nothing could make him happy. The first couple of years of our marriage I bent over backward to do whatever I could to make him not complain, but then I gave up. Either it was Harold's way or no way."

Sasha thought about what she'd had to go through to keep peace in her marriage. And like her mother, she had done whatever she could to make Grant happy, and despite his meteoric rise in country music, it was never enough for him. If she'd had this conversation with Charlotte before she'd exchanged vows with Grant, Sasha knew she would not have married him. However, she wasn't one to live with regrets, because it taught her what she would or would not accept if or when she became involved with a man again.

"You really like Dwight, don't you, Mama?"

Charlotte smiled. "What is there not to like, Natasha? He's gorgeous, intelligent and a wonderful father. You can tell in a single glance that he dotes on his daughter. Some men in his position would have a gaggle of women trailing after him. And you should count your-self among the lucky ones, because I believe you're the first woman from The Falls he's dated since Adrienne Wheeler."

"It could be he's not really into local women."

"Not into them how, Natasha?"

"Once burned, twice shy. Maybe he's afraid to com-mit to one again."

"Does that bother you?" Charlotte asked.

"No. I don't have a problem dating Dwight and not wanting more."

"What if it becomes more?"

"I can't and don't want to project that far into the future, Mama."

Sasha turned off into the driveway and parked be-side the van with the sweet shop's logo painted on the front doors. When she'd left earlier that afternoon to drive to Dwight's house to share Sunday dinner with him and his family, she never could've imagined that he would ask her to accompany him to a local social event. But first they would start tongues wagging when they showed up together at the Wolf Den. And going out with Dwight had taken care of one concern for her: he was willing to date women out of his race.

Charlotte opened the passenger-side door. "I think I'm going to turn in early. Right now, I'm as full as a tick, and after a couple of glasses of wine I doubt I'll be able to keep my eyes open long enough to watch my regular shows."

"Make that two stuffed ticks." Sasha got out and plucked the bag with containers of leftover food Vic-toria had insisted they take home with them once she'd sheepishly admitted she had cooked too much and didn't want it to go to waste.

Charlotte slowly made her way up the steps to the front door. "What are your plans for tomorrow?"

"First, I'm going to sleep in late. And then I'm going to the bank to deposit last week's receipts. I also plan to stop by the newspaper's office to see if Langston is there to interview me for his Who's Who column. We've been playing phone tag for a couple of weeks."

"You don't plan to go into the shop?"

Sasha shook her head. Although she closed Sunday and Monday, she would occasionally go in and put up batches of yeast for bread or doughnuts or roll out piecrusts. "No."

"Good. It's time you stop working when the shop is closed, or you'll end up burning out."

"As soon as I put the food away, I'm going to change into my jammies, get into bed and set the TV to sleep mode."

True to her word, Sasha stored the leftovers in the fridge, cleansed her face of makeup and got into a pair of pajamas and slipped into bed. Picking up the remote on the bedside table, she flicked on the television resting on its own stand and settled down to watch a pre-programmed romantic-comedy movie.

Sasha finished totaling the weekly receipts and entered the amount into a bookkeeping program on the laptop linked to the desktop in the shop. After disbursing payroll and paying vendors, the business had yielded a profit for the third consecutive week, alleviating some of her former anxiety that the bakeshop would not be sustainable. She'd projected six continuous months of profits before contacting cooking schools to solicit their recommendations for an assistant pastry chef.

Gathering her tote, she walked out of her bedroom and headed for the staircase. The sounds of laughter from the audience of a morning talk show came from the kitchen. The results of a positive checkup from her cardiologist was good news for Charlotte. She'd volunteered to work longer hours, but Sasha rejected her suggestion. She wanted to wait until the fall before increasing Charlotte's hours.

"Mama, I'm leaving now."

"Okay, baby."

Sasha found an empty spot on the street far from the bank. Shopkeepers were sweeping and hosing down the sidewalks fronting their businesses. All the business establishments were shaded by black-and-white-striped awnings. She'd become a window-shopper in her own hometown, as she peered into the windows of the dry cleaner, Laundromat, pharmacy, hardware and department stores. As a child, the highlights of her Saturdays were when her mother went downtown, where they'd spent hours browsing and shopping for things they needed and a few they didn't. The residents of The Falls did not have to leave their town to shop, because everything they'd want was available in the four-block-long business district.

She walked into the bank and did not have to wait for a teller, who cheerfully greeted her. He'd just completed her transaction when Sasha heard someone call her name. Turning, she recognized a woman with whom she'd shared several classes in high school. Georgi, who was biracial, had inherited each of her parents' best traits. She had a café au lait complexion, delicate features with a sprinkling of freckles and natural curly reddish hair that she'd pulled back and secured in a ponytail.

"Georgi. How are you?" Sasha's smile faded when she stared at Georgina Powell's teeth. The gap that had been so much of her trademark smile was missing.

Georgina's large round eyes, the color of bright copper pennies, crinkled when she threw back her head and laughed. "I know you're shocked not to see the gap, but I decided to give myself a present for my thirtieth birthday, because that was the first thing folks noticed whenever I introduced myself."

Sasha managed to look sheepish. "I must admit it was very distinctive." Georgina had been an illustrator for their high school's newspaper, and she had always talked about becoming an artist, but knew that was wishful thinking because she was expected to work for and eventually take control of the department store that had been in the Powell family for more than four generations. It had started up at the turn of the previous century as a general store selling everything from feed, seeds, fabric and household tools to canned goods. It expanded for years until it stocked enough merchandise that residents did not have to seek out large box or chain stores lining the interstate.

"I heard a couple of months ago that you were back in The Falls, but I've been up to my eyeballs helping out my parents at the store that I don't even have time to breathe. Stocking shelves, keeping track of inventory and taking care of customers has become a bit overwhelming. You should know that now that you're running your own business."

"It can be somewhat daunting at times, but thankfully I have my mother, who has been a blessing."

Georgina leaned closer. "That's what I want to talk to you about whenever you have some free time."

"Do you want to give me a hint?" Sasha asked.

"I'm thinking of opening my own business here in The Falls."

Somewhat taken aback, Sasha went completely still. "You intend to compete with your parents for business?"

Georgina shook her head. "I definitely will not compete. My father has decided to downsize the arts-and-crafts section and I want to open a small shop featuring needlecrafts. I'm aware that it may be a dying art, but there are a lot of folks who still knit and crochet. I also plan to give classes for those who want to learn to quilt by hand or machine. I used to complain when my grandmother forced me to learn needlecrafts, but now I'm grateful that she did. When she passed away, she left me a collection of quilts dating back to before the Civil War."

"They have to be priceless." Sasha was unable to disguise the awe in her voice.

"They are. We'll talk about that another time. Right now, I need to deposit these receipts and get back to the store."

"Call the shop and let me know when you're available."

Georgina hugged Sasha. "Thanks, girl."

Sasha walked out of the bank, wondering why her former classmate wasn't pursuing her dream of becoming an illustrator instead of planning to open a needlecraft shop. Georgina wasn't just talented; she was gifted.

Reuniting with Georgina reminded Sasha that she

was still estranged from her hometown. She'd returned the summer before and today was the first time she'd strolled along Main Street and gone into the bank, because normally Charlotte did that.

Once Sasha had made the decision to return to Wickham Falls, she did not call and tell her mother. When she rang the bell and Charlotte opened the door, Sasha knew she'd looked vastly different than she had during her last visit, but she was also different inwardly. The first few weeks were a repeat of the one before: she slept, ate and watched countless movies. Then one day she decided she'd hidden enough and went into Preston McAvoy's office to file papers of incorporation for her proposed new business. With her distinctive red hair dyed a nondescript brown and her face hidden by oversize sunglasses, no one recognized her as the woman who'd been married to the Nashville recording artist who'd crossed over from country to pop and Southern rock. Sasha had managed to keep a low profile even after word spread that she'd filed a permit to open a shop in the downtown business district.

She knew her customers were curious as to why she had come back and even more so why she'd decided to divorce her superstar husband and give up what had been a glamorous lifestyle. Having her mother and Kiera man the front of the shop had saved Sasha from answering questions she had no intention of explaining.

She was certain being seen with Dwight would generate more than its share of gossip, but at this point in her life Sasha was past caring what people thought of her. It had taken years for her to come into her own, and now at thirty-two she liked what she had become: the captain of her own destiny.

* * *

Dwight drove onto the driveway to the Manning house and got out. He had questioned himself over and over if he was courting trouble dating his daughter's employer; the last local woman he'd dated he married, and despite his attraction to Sasha, he had no intention of marrying her or any other woman—at least for several years. He'd always mapped out his future carefully and it was only because of unforeseen circumstances that he was forced to modify his plans.

The door opened before he could ring the bell and he came face-to-face with the subject of his musings. The sensual scent of her perfume, which now he could recognize if he was in a room with dozens of women. Sasha did not even remotely resemble the women he'd been involved with since his divorce, but that did not detract from what he'd found so engaging about her. She'd occasionally exhibit a shyness whenever he looked at her too long, making him wonder if she'd had much experience with men. Kiera constantly talked about her in glowing terms, which only made her go up several points on his approval scale.

"You look very nice."

It was the only thing Dwight could think to say when he noticed the black stretchy long-sleeved T-shirt Sasha had paired with matching leggings and low-heel booties. The black attire, hugging every curve of her slim figure, made her appear even taller. She'd styled her hair in a ponytail and applied a light cover of makeup to her eyes and mouth. Sasha lowered her eyes, gazing up at him through long charcoal-gray lashes, a sensual gesture he'd come to recognize and look for.

"Thank you. I'll be right with you. I just have to get my jacket and keys."

Dwight turned his back rather than stare at the sensual sway of Sasha's hips in the body-hugging attire. He had an inkling that Sasha was totally unaware of how sexy she was, and because of this he had to be very careful not to cross or blur the lines going from friends to lovers. Sleeping with her would not only complicate their relationship, but it would also impact Sasha and Kiera's. He shook his head as if to banish any licentious thoughts.

"Ready." Sasha had returned, wearing a fatigue jacket. "It's an old one that belonged to one of my brothers."

A knowing smile tugged at the corners of Dwight's mouth. All former and present members of the different branches were required to wear military paraphernalia to take advantage of the advertised specials at the sports bar. "Let's go, Corporal Manning."

Sasha glanced down at her brother's name and rank stamped on the jacket. "Maybe I should exchange it for another one."

Dwight took her hand. "Please don't. Everyone knows you belong to a military family." He led her around the passenger side of the Jeep and assisted her up.

"Why did you decide to join the army?" Sasha asked as he got in and sat beside her.

He gave a quick glance. "I wanted to continue the tradition of serving that began in my family dating back to before the Spanish–American War. Some of my relatives were buffalo soldiers, and before that served in all-black regiments during the Civil War."

"What if you'd decided not to serve?"

Dwight put the vehicle in gear and drove down the

tree-lined street, heading in the direction of the local road leading to the Wolf Den. "That wasn't an option. I grew up listening to my father and grandfather trade war stories about Korea and Vietnam, and for me it was like watching a war movie. I'd heard the term 'shell shock,' but it wasn't until I was much older that I realized it was a form of PTSD."

"Why did you decide to become a dentist?"

"It really wasn't my first choice. When I'd enrolled in college as a premed student, I'd planned to become a pediatrician. It wasn't until my junior year that I decided I wanted to become a dentist."

"Do you like being a dentist?"

"I love it. I like the personal one-on-one contact with the patient sitting in my chair, and helping people achieve a healthy mouth, which is essential to overall good health, is very satisfying."

"Do you think Kiera wants to become a dentist?"

Coming to a stop at a four-way intersection, Dwight looked for oncoming traffic. "She hasn't said anything to me about it. Right now, all she talks about is learning to make fancy cakes." He knew he'd shocked Sasha with this disclosure when she emitted an audible gasp.

"Has she actually told you she wants to become a pastry chef?" Sasha asked.

"Not in so many words," he replied truthfully. Dwight didn't want to tell Sasha that his daughter talked non-stop about the customers that came into the sweet shop and about her employer.

"Would it bother you if she did choose a career as a pastry chef?"

Dwight shook his head. "No. I've asked my daughter what she wants to be when she grows up, and she always says she doesn't know. What I don't want to do is put pressure on her as to her career choice. I tell her that once she decides, it should be something she's passionate about. But what I will not do is support her if she wants to become a professional student because she doesn't know what she wants to be."

"Her wanting to learn to bake may be just a phase, but I'm willing to give her lessons once I hire an assistant. That probably won't be until the summer. Even if she elects not to become a pastry chef, she can always use it as a backup to supplement her income."

"Did you know that you were going to be a pastry chef when you graduated high school?"

Sasha paused. "That's a long story. I'll tell you about it at another time."

Dwight registered something in Sasha's tone that indicated it was something she truly did not want to talk about, and he was perceptive enough not to bring up the topic again. After all, they were still more strangers than friends.

He maneuvered off the local road and down a sloping decline to a path leading through a copse of trees before the landscape opened to a valley as the Wolf Den came into view. The mouthwatering aroma of smoked meats wafted through partially open windows of the Jeep. A smokehouse and newly erected red-painted barn were located behind the restaurant. The Den's owners had built the barn to double as a venue for catered affairs. It was the only business in town with a license to serve alcohol. The parking lot alongside the building was crowded with SUVs and pickups, and a few Harleys. He pulled into a reserved space bearing his name and rank.

Sasha gave him an incredulous look at the same time she undid her seat belt. "You get your own parking space?"

Dwight winked at her. "Only on Military Monday. As the highest-ranking officer in The Falls, I'm afforded the honor."

Her smile matched his. "So, rank does have its privileges."

He nodded. "Yes, it does." The owners had afforded him the privilege after town council members voted to host Community Week for residents to volunteer to give back or pay it forward. Dwight had elected to treat all active, retired and/or former military personnel free of charge, regardless of whether they had dental insurance. "Don't move. I'll help you down."

Sasha waited for Dwight to get out and open her door. He extended his arms and she slid off the seat as he held her effortlessly, her head level with his for several seconds, before lowering her until her feet touched the ground. Suddenly, she felt light-headed, as if she couldn't draw a normal breath because they were a hairbreadth away from each other. Being this close to Dwight made her feel as if she'd been sucked into a vortex that made everything around her vanish like a puff of smoke. Ripples of awareness eddied through her, and for the first time in a very long time she felt a longing that she wanted to be made love to. However, she knew realistically that couldn't happen. There was no way she was going to become physically involved with the father of her employee. It would not bode well for her, Dwight or Kiera if they decided to break up.

And in that instant, she knew it was best for them to become friends.

Friends without benefits.

"Let's go in so that we can give these folks something to talk about."

Reaching over her head, Dwight shut the door and then held her hand and led her out of the parking lot to the front of the eating establishment.

Chapter Six

Sasha had grown up listening to stories about the celebrated sports bar, but this was her first time stepping foot into the place that had earned the reputation of serving the best smoked meat in the county. The ear-shattering sounds of raised voices, the waitstaff shouting food orders and the deep, pulsing music from a heavy-metal band coming from hidden speakers were an assault on her senses.

A crowd of men and women were standing two-deep at the bar, where a trio of bartenders were filling drink orders. Although the legal drinking age in West Virginia was twenty-one, the owners of the Wolf Den had posted a sign stating they reserved the right not to serve anyone under twenty-three. More than a half dozen wall-mounted muted televisions were tuned to sporting events.

"Attention!" Everyone went completely still, and all manner of speech ended abruptly as they executed salutes. Sasha also froze when she saw everyone staring at her and Dwight.

"At ease, everyone." Dwight's voice, though low, carried easily above the music.

It suddenly dawned on Sasha the assembly had acknowledged him as a senior ranking officer. Going on tiptoe, she whispered close to his ear, "Does this always happen when you come in?"

Dwight lowered his head and pressed his mouth to her hair. "It started as a joke a couple of years ago and it stuck. Anyone who was or is a commissioned officer gets the spotlight." His hand rested at the small of her back. "Let me see if I can find a table before we can order something to eat."

Sasha glanced around the sports bar. Almost everyone wore an article of clothing advertising a branch of the military. She stared at a tray a waitress balanced on her shoulder filled with dishes of grilled meat and sides. The mouthwatering aroma of brisket, chicken, ribs and baked beans with pieces of burnt ends, collard greens, and macaroni and cheese wafted to her nostrils. Wrapping her arm around Dwight's waist, she moved even closer to him when the door opened, and more people came in.

"Doc Adams! Over here!"

Dwight craned his neck to see who was calling his name. He spied one of the owners beckoning him closer. Tonight Aiden Gibson, a former navy SEAL, was doing double duty as the pit master and bartender. Resting his hand at the small of Sasha's back, he shouldered his way through the throng to find two stools at the far end of the bar.

A network of fine lines fanned out around Aiden's blue-green eyes when he smiled. "I wasn't certain whether you would show up tonight. I'll have one of the waitstaff get a table for you."

Dwight seated Sasha and then reached over the bar and shook Aiden's hand. "Thanks for looking out for us. Aiden, I'm not certain whether you know Sasha Manning." He studied her delicate profile. "Sasha, Aiden Gibson. He happens to be one of the owners of this fine dining establishment."

Sasha extended her hand. "It's a pleasure to meet you."

Aiden cradled her much smaller hand in his. "I'm more familiar with your brother Phil, because he and I were in some of the same classes. Aren't you the cake lady everyone's talking about?" A slight flush suffused Sasha's fair complexion as she modestly inclined her head. "You and I have to talk at another time, because I'm thinking of adding a few items to our dessert menu. Now, what can I get you good folks to drink while you wait for a table?"

Dwight dropped an arm over Sasha's shoulders. "What do you want, sweetie?" The endearment had just slipped out.

She stared at the chalkboard with the day's specials and beers. "I'll have a Blue Moon."

He ordered Sasha's beer and a Dos Equis for himself. Minutes later, Aiden placed pint glasses of ice-cold beer on two coasters. Raising his glass, Dwight touched it to Sasha's, which was garnished with an orange slice. "Enjoy."

She took a long swallow of her icy brew, moaning softly. "That's nice."

Picking up a napkin, Dwight gently held her chin and blotted the froth off her upper lip. He leaned closer and brushed his mouth over hers, savoring the lingering taste of orange. "We need to make folks believe we're a couple," he whispered against her moist parted lips. Although not prone to displays of public affection, Dwight admitted to himself that he enjoyed kissing Sasha.

Sasha looked up at him through her lashes. "You're right." The two words were barely off her tongue when she leaned closer and kissed him on the mouth, the joining lasting almost five seconds. "I think that's a lot more convincing."

Dwight felt the flesh between his thighs stir to life, and he pressed his knees tightly together as he struggled not to become fully aroused. He cursed to himself when he realized he'd concocted a dangerous scheme that backfired. He'd convinced himself he and Sasha could see each other socially without a physical entanglement. Now it was apparent he was wrong because his body had just reminded him how long it had been since he'd been intimately involved with a woman; his last relationship, by mutual agreement, did not include sharing a bed.

Sitting straight, he saw Sasha staring back at him. It was impossible for him to read her expression. "Are you okay?"

A mysterious smile softened Sasha's mouth. "I'm more than okay."

And she was. Kissing Dwight, really kissing him, had assuaged her curiosity about the man whose image plagued her days and nights. She hadn't had a lot of experience when it came to the opposite sex, but after almost five years of marriage to a narcissist, she'd come to know what she did not like or want in a man.

Sasha knew she wasn't a girl, but a woman, who no longer entertained fantasies about finding her prince who would sweep her away and they would live happily ever after. Her grandmother had given her a colorful cloth-covered journal for her eighth birthday with a note for her to write down everything that had happened to her that day and every day thereafter. She told her that she had to be honest about her feelings, because the entries would provide a blueprint as to how she should live her life.

It wasn't until years later, when she unpacked the personal belongings she'd shipped from Nashville to Wickham Falls, that Sasha found the journals. She'd kept them because they were the last link between her and her grandmother; she sat in bed and read every entry. Her childish print gave way to a beautiful cursive along with drawings that hinted of the artistic ability she would eventually use when designing cakes.

When she compared Dwight to Grant, she realized they were complete opposites in appearance and personality. She'd found Dwight even-tempered, generous and affectionate, while Grant was critical, opinionated and selfish. It was only when Grant was in public or onstage performing for a crowd that he was able to morph into the charming, magnetic man women fantasized about and men wanted to be.

"Hey, Sasha. What are you doing here?"

She turned to find someone she hadn't seen since their high school graduation. Gregg Henderson had been her prom date. He wore a tan-colored T-shirt under a desert fatigue jacket. "What happened to 'how are you?'" she teased, smiling.

Gregg ran a hand over his close-cropped sandy-brown hair. His dark blue eyes in a deeply tanned face reminded her of sapphires. "Sorry about that." He leaned closer and kissed her cheek. "How are you?"

"I'm well. And how have you been?"

"I'm really good. I just finished my second tour, so I'm going to be stateside for a while. My mother told me about you marrying and then divorcing that country singer. What happened?"

Sasha's expression changed, becoming a mask of stone. "We decided to go our separate ways." She had no intention of giving Gregg the intimate details of her failed marriage.

"I'm going to be here for another couple of weeks, so maybe we can hang out together and catch up on old times."

She wanted to tell Gregg that there were no old times. He was the first boy to ask her to prom and she'd accepted. "I don't think that's going to be possible. When I'm not running my business, I try to spend time with my boyfriend." The moment she'd referred to Dwight as her boyfriend, Sasha knew for certain everyone in The Falls would know about it because Gregg's mother was an incurable gossipmonger.

"I didn't know you were seeing someone."

Looping her arm through Dwight's and resting her head on his shoulder, Sasha wordlessly confirmed to Gregg that she was seeing The Falls' resident dentist.

Gregg's eyes were large as silver dollars when he realized who she was talking about. "I suppose I'll see you around." Turning, he walked away, leaving Sasha staring at his back.

"You played that off quite well."

Sasha looked at Dwight, who appeared to have an intense interest in the plastic-covered menu. "I suppose you heard everything."

"Curious and wondering how you were going to handle him coming on to you."

"He really wasn't coming on to me, Dwight."

Dwight's inky-black eyebrows rose. "You think not? He was talking about catching up on old times."

"The old times was prom. He was my prom date and nothing beyond that."

"You didn't date him in high school?"

Sasha lowered her eyes. Dwight was asking a question that if she answered would open a Pandora's box of memories she'd put behind her. "I didn't date anyone in high school." He gave her an incredulous look. "I didn't want any entanglements when I knew I was leaving town following graduation."

She'd told Dwight a half lie. If she'd had a boyfriend, she knew he probably would've tried to convince her to stay. At the time she knew she had to put some distance between her and her parents before she had a complete mental breakdown.

"Why did you leave, Sasha?"

"That's a long story. One that I can't talk about *here*."

Dwight dropped a kiss on her hair. "Forgive me for prying."

"There's nothing to forgive, sweetie," she whispered, repeating his term of endearment. "I want to thank you."

"For what?"

"For masquerading as my boyfriend because I don't

need or want a repeat of what I just had with Gregg. I've discovered some men don't react well to rejection."

Once she'd appeared on the competition cooking show she was easily recognizable because of her distinctive laugh and red hair. At the time she didn't know whether men were attracted to her because she'd become a celebrity chef, or if they liked her for herself, which resulted in her deftly rejecting any offers to take her out. She'd had one serious relationship before Grant, which had ended badly. He had been one of her culinary school instructors. Almost fifteen years her senior, he did not deal well with rejection, and she was forced to move out of her apartment once he began stalking her. It ended only when she reported him to the police; the judge warned him that a subsequent arrest could result in his serving time in prison.

Dwight threaded their fingers together, bringing her hand to his mouth and kissing the back of it. "I think I'm going to enjoy masquerading as your boyfriend."

She gazed into a pair of dark eyes that reminded her of tiny cups of espresso. Light from pendants shimmered on the cropped salt-and-pepper strands covering his head, while casting long and short shadows over Dwight's exquisitely sculpted face. It wasn't for the first time that she wondered why some woman hadn't gotten him to fall in love and marry her, despite his pronouncement that he liked being single. Sasha was preempted from replying when a waitress came over to inform them she had an available table for them.

Dwight ordered for himself and Sasha. Once the dishes arrived and she bit into a succulent piece of smoked brisket, she said she now knew why the Wolf

Den was so popular with folks in The Falls and surrounding towns. He introduced her to men and women—some with whom she was familiar and others who were complete strangers. It was apparent she'd missed a lot during her fourteen-year absence.

The time was approaching nine when a waitress came over to the table to ask him if he wanted another beer. "No, thank you. But I will take the check."

Sasha touched the napkin to her mouth. "Is there anybody in town that you don't know?" she asked, teasingly.

"Very few. Remember, I've lived here all my life. Even when I went to college and dental school, I managed to come back in between semesters." He looked at something over her head. "There's something about Wickham Falls that keeps pulling me back whenever I'm away for any appreciable period of time."

"Maybe it's because you had a very happy childhood."

Dwight's eyes narrowed suspiciously. "And you didn't?"

Sasha's eyelids fluttered wildly. "It wasn't as happy as it should've been. My parents argued."

"What parents don't, Sasha?"

"Every day, Dwight."

He stood, signaled for the waitress and handed her three large bills. "Keep the change." Rounding the booth, he cupped Sasha's elbow, helping her to stand. "Let's go, Cinderella. I promised to get you home by nine."

Dwight escorted her out of the restaurant and into the cool night air. Sasha's mentioning her parents arguing every day was certain to negatively impact her attitude about relationships. Had she and her ex-husband quarreled so much that it had put a strain on their marriage until it resulted in divorce?

He wanted to tell Sasha that he and Adrienne rarely argued until it came time for him to set up his practice. Then it was relentless and uncompromising. What he could not and did not understand at the time was why she so vehemently objected when she'd known for years of his intentions. However, once they were divorced and she moved to New York and reunited with one of her college classmates, realization dawned for Dwight. Adrienne finally admitted that she'd had an affair with the man who would eventually become her second husband.

Sasha attempted to stifle a yawn as he drove out of the parking lot. "Sleepy or full?"

"Both," she admitted, smiling. "Thank you for inviting me to come with you."

"Anytime."

"How often do you come for Military Monday?"

"I try to make it at least once and no more than twice a month. I really like hanging out at the lake house."

"What you really like is fishing."

Dwight gave Sasha a quick glance. "Yup. It's the only thing I like better than dentistry." A beat passed, and then he asked, "Do you fish?"

"Some."

"How much is some, Sasha?"

"Just say I've learned to fly-fish."

Dwight's teeth shone whitely in the glow of the illumination coming from the dashboard. "Are you saying you've mastered the wrist action?"

"Some," Sasha repeated.

"We'll have to see how much 'some' you have if you ever decide to join Kiera and me at the lake."

"How about your mother? Does she ever join you?"

"She did when I first bought the place, but she's not much for roughing it."

"Does roughing it translate into bathing in the lake?" Sasha questioned.

"Nah," Dwight said, laughing. "The house has all the comforts of home with indoor plumbing, hot and cold running water, electricity, heat and air-conditioning. There are quite a few retirees who live there year-round."

"How secluded is it?"

"Just say you have to know where you're going to find it. Anytime you need a break and want to escape for a day or two, just let me know and I'll make it happen."

"It sounds tempting."

Dwight heard the hesitation in her voice and wondered if she thought he had an ulterior motive for inviting her. "The cabin has two bedrooms, and there's also a loft that sleeps a third person."

"I'll definitely think about it."

"My invitation comes with no strings attached, and because of this I promise you nothing physical can ever happen between us."

"Do you really find me so unattractive that I repulse you that much? I constantly overhear customers that come into the shop tell Kiera that she's a beauty just like her mother."

Dwight did not want to believe what had just come out of Sasha's mouth as his hands tightened on the steering wheel. "Your ex must have really done a number on you if you believe you're not an attractive woman, Sasha."

"Leave my ex out of this."

"Why?" he countered.

"Because I don't want to talk about him."

Signaling, Dwight maneuvered off the road and came to a stop where he would be out of the path of coming traffic. Shifting into Park, he unbuckled his seat belt and turned to look at Sasha. "We don't have to talk about him, but I think we need to straighten out a few details so you can understand where I'm coming from." Her eyes appeared abnormally large as she stared at him. Reaching over, he rested his hand on the nape of her neck, his fingertips pressed against the runaway pulse. "You don't have to concern yourself with me trying to get you to go to bed with me, and it's not because I don't find you attractive. But our sleeping together would only complicate things for both of us. My daughter works for you and the situation could become somewhat awkward if or when we broke up."

Sasha was mute for a full minute as she replayed what Dwight had just told her. She'd asked him if he'd found her unattractive because whenever she was out with Grant, he would compare her to other women he'd claim he found more beautiful. And to a small-town girl who rarely wore makeup and bought her clothes off the rack, Sasha had always believed she would never be able to compete with the more glamorous wives of the other recording stars. Even after she hired a dresser who selected her clothes and a makeup artist taught her what to use to enhance her best features, the insecurities lingered.

She did not want to talk about her ex-husband, because she couldn't. She'd signed a nondisclosure agreement not to divulge the details of their marriage because to do so could negatively impact the wholesome country-boy image his publicist had created for him. Only her mother knew, after she'd sworn her to secrecy, what she'd had to go through during her five-year marriage.

"I only asked if you found me unattractive because I know how everyone talks about how beautiful Kiera's mother is," she lied smoothly.

Dwight's fingertips feathered over the column of her neck. "It's not about how a woman looks on the outside, Sasha. Some women are like an apple—beautiful on the outside, but once you bite into it you discover it's rotten to the core. You're one of those rare finds who's beautiful inside and out."

Sasha didn't know if Dwight was telling her she was beautiful because he thought that was what she wanted to hear, yet there was something in his voice and reassuring touch that lessened her despair and filled her with a sense of strength she didn't know she had. Something unknown communicated that Dwight was good to and for her even if they never became lovers. He had proved that during the time they'd spent at the Wolf Den. She'd found him attentive and protective whenever a man appeared to express an interest in her. He would place a proprietary arm around her shoulders or kiss her hair, silently signaling she wasn't available.

She'd admitted to her mother that one day if or when she married again it would be for love, and having Dwight as a friend was a bonus, given her dearth of experience when it came to men. She'd slept with one man before

Grant, and if or when she slept with the next one, she prayed it would be her last.

Sasha rested her head on Dwight's shoulder. "You are so good for a woman's ego."

"It's about the truth and not my attempting to boost your ego, Sasha. I've been divorced a lot longer than you have, so it's going to be a while before you stop blaming yourself for what you did or didn't do."

A trembling smile parted her lips. "You think?"

"I know," he said confidently. "Now, it's time I get you home so you can get your beauty rest."

Sasha wanted to tell Dwight that not only was he good for her, but also good to her. He was the first man who'd treated her like an equal, and for that she was grateful. The man she'd given her virginity to would go into jealous rages and reprimand her like a father with a child whenever he'd believed she wasn't being attentive enough. And she did not want to think about Grant, who calculatingly found ways to emotionally abuse her because he'd believed there wasn't enough room in their marriage for two celebrities.

Dwight secured his seat belt and the remainder of the drive was completed in silence, and when he maneuvered into the driveway to her home, Sasha knew she wasn't the same person she'd been when she'd opened the door for him. She waited for him to come around and help her down.

"Thank you for a wonderful time."

Dwight angled his head. "Does this mean you want to do it again?"

Sasha smiled. "Of course. And I'll let you know when I'm ready to go fly-fishing with you and Kiera."

"That's a bet."

"Good night, Dwight."

"Good night, Sasha. I'll text you later in the week about when to expect me to pick you up for the dinner dance."

"Okay." She turned and walked up the steps to the house, unlocked the door, and then closed and locked it behind her.

"How did it go?"

Sasha turned to find her mother in a nightgown and bathrobe standing in the middle of the living room holding a glass of water. "How did what go?"

"Your date with Dwight."

Bending slightly, Sasha kicked off her shoes. "It really wasn't a date."

"I'm not so old that I don't know when a man comes to a woman's home to take her out that it's a date."

"All right, Mama. It was a date. And it was perfect."

"That's all I need to know. Good night."

Sasha watched her mother walk across the living room to the staircase. "Good night, Mama. By the way, do you want to know if he kissed me?"

Charlotte stopped halfway. "No. That's too much information. Don't stay up too late."

Sasha smiled. "I won't."

She'd planned to be in bed by ten. Her workday usually began between five and six in the morning and ended twelve hours later. And now that Aiden Gibson wanted her to bake for the Den, she knew hiring an assistant sooner rather than later was now a priority. As she climbed the staircase to the second story, she smiled when she thought about the hours she'd spent with Dwight. And she'd been truthful with her mother when she admitted it was a date and that it was perfect.

And as perfect as she found Dwight, Sasha realized she could not afford to lose focus. Not when she needed all her energy to grow her business.

Dwight sat up in bed with a mound of pillows cradling his back and shoulders, staring at the images on the flat screen. It was past midnight and he knew he should've been sleeping instead of watching the encore of basketball playoff games.

After dropping Sasha off, he'd come home to find a note from his mother that Kiera had decided to stay with her rather than have a sleepover with the neighbor's daughter. He wondered what Victoria had said or done to entice her granddaughter to sleep in the guesthouse. Dwight had given up completely lecturing Victoria about turning into the indulgent grandparent as she attempted to give or take Kiera whatever and wherever she wanted.

Against his protestations, Victoria had gifted Kiera with a pair of diamond studs, totaling two carats, for her sixteenth birthday. The earrings had been a gift to her from her husband for their twentieth wedding anniversary. He much would've preferred his mother give his daughter a strand of her pearls, but Victoria overrode him when she said it was her right to give her only grandchild whatever she wanted. Dwight had not missed his mother's backhanded reminder that her only child had elected to give her only one grandchild. However, it wasn't his mother or daughter that kept him from going to sleep but Sasha. He couldn't stop thinking about what he'd said to her about their not sleeping together.

Was he attracted to her? The answer was yes.

He'd asked himself did he like her, and again the answer was a resounding yes.

But the defining question was the probability of his sleeping with her. And if he were truly honest, his body said yes while his head said no.

Dwight realized his ambivalence about Sasha stemmed from two factors: she was his daughter's employer, and she lived in Wickham Falls. He wasn't bothered if they were seen together out and about because they were friends—without benefits. What he couldn't understand was Sasha believing he'd found her unattractive, and he wondered if she was conscious of the differences in their race, and of the fact that Adrienne, at the age of sixteen, had won a beauty contest.

Well, the quiet, talented redhead did not have to concern herself about her appearance. What she failed to realize was that not only was she cute, but she claimed an understated sexiness he found appealing.

Picking up the remote device, he turned off the television and rearranged the pillows, so he lay in a more comfortable position. Sleep was slow in coming, and when it did, he temporarily forgot about the sweetness of Sasha's mouth when they kissed; the subtle hypnotic scent of her perfume that had lingered in the Jeep when she was no longer there. But an image of the way she innocently lowered her eyes and glanced up at him through her lashes visited him in an erotic dream. It served as a reminder of how long it had been since he'd slept with a woman.

Chapter Seven

Sasha felt like the hamster she saw in a pet shop running around on a wheel until he finally collapsed from exhaustion. She was overtired and close to burnout. Even when she'd sat at Adele Harvey's bedside around the clock for three days, leaving only to shower and change her clothes, she hadn't felt this fatigued.

Aiden Gibson, as promised, had called her to place an order for six cakes: coconut cream, bourbon-pecan pound, German chocolate, chocolate-raspberry truffle, strawberry cheesecake and red velvet.

Langston Cooper had come by the shop to inquire when she would be available for an interview, and again she told him she did not have the time. She had also put off meeting with Georgina Powell with the excuse that if Georgi came by her house late in the evening, she would set aside time for them to talk. She had just finished decorating the last of three dozen cupcakes with colorful tulips for a mother who wanted to take them to school for her daughter's eighth birthday when Kiera entered the kitchen.

"Miss Sasha, there's a Miss Campos asking to see you."

"Tell her I'll be right there." She set down the piping bag and discarded the disposable gloves. Using Russian piping tips to create leaves and colorful flowers, she'd decorated all the cupcakes in less than ten minutes. Pressed for time, Sasha had called in her prior experience when she'd been a contestant in a timed competition.

Sasha walked into the front of the shop to find Nicole Campos sitting at one of the three bistro tables. She now could count on regular customers who came in most mornings to order coffee and the daily special. It seemed so long ago that she'd come to Preston McAvoy's office to retain the attorney to file an application to set up a corporation. She knew Nicole was just as shocked to see her as she was to discover that Nicole now worked for the law firm.

She took a chair opposite Nicole, immediately noticing obvious changes in the woman who'd attained the rank of captain in the Corps piloting Black Hawk helicopter gunships. Her face was fuller than when she last saw her, and her hair had grown out of the pixie cut. Even her tawny-brown complexion was darker, as if she'd spent time in the sun.

"Congratulations on your engagement." Word had traveled quickly around The Falls that Fletcher Austen and Nicole had gotten engaged. And she could count on her mother to keep her abreast of local gossip. Charlotte tended to talk to everyone who came into the shop.

Nicole's eyes went to the diamond ring on her left hand, as a slight blush further darkened her delicate features. "Thank you."

"Have you set a date?"

Nicole nodded. "Yes. That's why I've come to see you about a wedding cake."

"When do you need it?" Sasha asked.

Lowering her eyes, Nicole focused on her outstretched hands. "A week from this coming Saturday. I know it's short notice," she said quickly. "But Fletcher is insisting we marry before I start showing."

"You're pregnant." The query had come out like a statement.

Nicole nodded again. "I just completed my first trimester, and even though I'm willing to wait until after I have the baby to get married, Fletcher says he doesn't want to be labeled a baby daddy."

Good for him, Sasha mused. There were some men in town who had chosen not to marry the women who'd had their children, preferring instead to live their lives by their leave. Fletcher Austen, a former decorated soldier, had become a much sought-after bachelor once he returned to civilian life to work in his family-owned auto repair business.

"How many people are you inviting?" It would be the first wedding cake she would bake since opening the shop.

Nicole shrugged under the suit jacket she'd put on over a white cotton man-tailored shirt. "I'm not sure. Fletcher keeps adding folks to the list, so right now it's anyone's guess. Of course, our families are invited, but then he began contacting some of the people he served with. I didn't want to be outdone, so I invited some of my buddies from the Corps. He just told me this morning that he's also invited everyone who hangs out at the Den on Military Monday."

Sasha did not envy Nicole, and she wondered if Dwight had received an invitation. She knew what went into planning a wedding, but to continually add names to the guest list was certain to create premarital problems. "I need a ballpark figure, Nicole. Fifty. Seventy-five."

Nicole threw up her hands. "Make it a hundred. I'd rather have too much than not enough. I refuse to let this wedding stress me out. I intend to show up, say my vows, eat, dance, and then go to bed and sleep until nature or hunger force me to get up."

Sasha laughed. "Where do you plan to hold the wedding and reception?"

"Everything will be done at the house. We've already ordered a tent, tables, chairs, DJ, and the Gibsons are going to cater the food. I told Fletcher I want simplicity and not some catering hall where people have to get all dressed up."

"Come into the back with me, where we can talk about what type of cake you want." Sasha smiled at Kiera, who'd just handed a customer a box filled with an assortment of muffins she'd baked earlier that morning. Most days she was able to sell out most of what she'd made that day. "Are you certain you don't want something to eat?" she asked Nicole again once they were seated in the area she'd set aside as her office.

"I just ate, so I'm good for another few hours."

Forty-five minutes later Sasha had entered every detail for the cake for the Campos-Fletcher nuptials into the desktop. Nicole had chosen a romantic look of pale pink hearts and flowers on tri-level stands, positioned at six, twelve and nineteen inches in height. Each cake, eight, ten and twelve inches in diameter, would serve at least one hundred guests. It took Nicole longer to select the cake, and eventually she decided on red velvet and carrot, both with cream-cheese fillings, and a classic white with confetti sprinkles.

Sasha quoted a price and the attorney handed her a credit card, and then gave her the address where she and Fletcher were living together. She was certain the wedding guests would be surprised to find the new flavor combinations under the delicate flowers and buttercream and royal icings.

There had been a time when she'd baked cakes exclusively for weddings, baby and bridal showers, anniversary and retirement dinners. Most of her clients wanted over-the-top creations to outdo one another. Sasha walked Nicole to the door before returning to the kitchen, where she checked her inventory for what she needed to make the cake. Although she liked baking muffins, cookies and bread, it was creating theme cakes that proved both most challenging and most rewarding. She returned to the shop's office to email several cooking schools to solicit a possible apprentice to assist now that her workload had increased.

It was after ten on a Friday night when Sasha sat on the front porch with Georgina, listening to her friend pour her heart out about wanting to open her own business without incurring her parents' wrath. They were expecting her to take over managing the department store once they retired.

"I sort of dropped a hint the other day and my mother went ballistic, telling me that I'm ungrateful, and that she and my father have sacrificed everything to keep the store afloat when they've had to compete with some of the larger department stores that went up on the interstate."

"Did you say anything about opening a shop in The Falls?"

Georgina shook her head and closed her eyes. "No, because knowing my father, he probably would tell the landlord not to rent it to me. Don't forget the Powell name goes a long way here in Wickham Falls."

Sasha nodded. Georgina's father could trace his ancestry back to the early seventeenth century, when they sailed from Wales for the Colonies. They'd started out as pig and sheep farmers and as merchants following the Civil War, when they opened a blacksmith shop and then a feed store and general store.

"Have you thought about setting up a shop in another town?" she asked.

Georgina gave Sasha an incredulous stare. "Did you when you opened your bakeshop?"

Sasha wanted to tell Georgina their conversation had nothing to do with her. "No."

"Why, Sasha?"

"I only asked because you may have to deal with interference from your parents. Meanwhile, there's just me and Mama, who was 100 percent behind me when I told her about my plans. But if you're looking to challenge your parents to prove your independence, then do it."

A silence ensued until Georgina said, "You're right about me wanting to be emancipated. I'm thirty-two years old and I've never left home. I can't find and keep a steady boyfriend once they discover I'm still living with my parents. One guy even told me that I was a child trapped in a woman's body."

Sasha grimaced. The remark may have been cruel, but she had to admit the man wasn't that far from the truth. At her age, Georgina needed to demonstrate a modicum of independence or she would spend the rest of her life either resenting her parents or blaming herself for not following her dreams. However, Sasha realized it wasn't easy to find enough strength to go through with changing one's life.

"What would you do if you were in my situation, Sasha?"

"Do you have your own money?" Georgina nodded. "The first thing I'd do is move out. Let them get used to not seeing you except when you come to the store."

Running a hand over her hair, Georgina tucked a wayward curl that had escaped the elastic band behind her right ear. "You're right." She paused. "Maybe I'll rent a place in Mineral Springs until I decide whether I want to live there permanently or move back to The Falls."

"That sounds like the beginning of a plan."

Sasha wondered if Georgina was serious about moving out of the house where she'd spent her entire life, or if saying it aloud made it sound more convincing. When most graduating seniors were planning the next phase of their lives to either enlist in the military, enroll in college, marry their high school sweethearts or seek employment outside of The Falls, Georgina had known exactly what she'd planned to do—work in Powell's Department Store. She knew Georgina's parents were devastated when their eldest son died from meningitis at the age of thirteen, which shifted the future responsibility of running the store to his younger sister.

Georgina stood. "I've taken up enough of your time talking about my crazy life."

Sasha rose to her feet and hugged her friend. "Anytime you need someone to talk to, just let me know." She smiled. "This too shall pass." She waited until Georgina drove away before going into the house and locking the door. Charlotte hadn't wanted her to move so far away, but there was nothing she could do or say to make her stay. She still remembered her father saying, *If she wants to leave, then let her go. My boys left, so why not my daughter?*

She never regretted leaving The Falls, marrying and divorcing Grant or returning home. It was as if her life had come full circle, and in doing so Sasha was content with her new life. She didn't have all the answers for Georgina except to offer moral support. And when she looked back, Sasha realized she had been a lot stronger at eighteen than her friend was now at thirty-two.

The following night was the chamber dinner dance, and because Sasha had an appointment with the local salon to have her hair trimmed Saturday afternoon, Charlotte had volunteered to work until closing. Earlier in the week, Dwight had sent her a text indicating he would pick her up at seven. The chamber had chosen to hold the event at the newly constructed barn behind the Wolf Den rather than in the ballroom at their favorite hotel off the interstate.

It had taken her a while to select a dress for the semi-formal affair among the ones she'd shipped back from Nashville. Those she'd worn when attending award ceremonies or social events with Grant she had donated to an organization set up to provide prom dresses to girls from needy families, and those with price tags she'd kept.

Sasha had admitted to Dwight that she was a country girl at heart, preferring going barefoot to wearing shoes. The only time she'd really dressed up was for prom, when Charlotte had driven her to a Charleston boutique where she could find a dress that had not come off the rack. She'd wanted only the best for her daughter's big night.

Now she was going to have another big night when she attended the fund-raiser as Dr. Dwight Adams's date. Sasha had been so busy during the week she hadn't had much time to think about her friend. And she'd come to think of him as her friend because she was pragmatic enough to know that friendship would be all they would ever share, no matter how much she wished for it to be otherwise.

Dwight knew he was gawking when Sasha opened the door. Like a butterfly emerging from its cocoon, she'd morphed into someone he wouldn't have recognized if it hadn't been for her hair and eye color. Smoky-brown shadow on her lids and red-gold waves floating around her face held him spellbound. How, he thought, could she have suggested that he did not find her attractive? But whether fresh-faced without a hint of makeup, or now wearing eye shadow, tangerine-orange lipstick, a hint of blush and the curls that were now loose waves, Dwight had been truthful when he told Sasha it wasn't about her looks but how they related to each other.

"You look incredible!"

The compliment had slipped out unbidden. The chocolate-brown off-the-shoulder dress with a revealing necklace was nipped at the waist and flowed out around her legs, drawing attention to Sasha's tall, slender body. His gaze traveled downward to a pair of brown, silk-covered strappy stilettos that put her close to his height of six foot two.

Smiling, Sasha held her arms out at her sides. "So, do I pass inspection, Major Adams?"

His smile was dazzling. "You're beyond anything I could've imagined, and I hope I don't have to rough up a few guys crazy enough to try to come on to my woman tonight."

Sasha's smile faded quickly. "Am I your woman, Dwight? I thought we were friends."

He took her hands, bringing them to his mouth and gently kissing the knuckles. "That, too. But, for the benefit of others, tonight you're my woman."

Sasha felt a chill sweep over her body despite the warmth of the late-spring night. Dwight didn't know how much she'd wanted to be his woman, girlfriend and lover if only to banish the pain she'd endured when married. But whenever she thought about a possible intimate relationship with Dwight, she did not want him to believe that she was using him to make up for what she hadn't had with Grant. Images of the many times when she'd argued with Grant only hours before they were scheduled to appear in public together came to mind and she shook her head as if to banish them.

Sasha forced a smile she didn't quite feel. She picked up the cashmere-and-silk shawl and small beaded evening bag off the table near the door. "I know it now." What she had to do was believe it. "I'm ready." And she was. Ready to enjoy whatever the night offered and her time with a man she was falling for when she'd told herself over and over they could not have a relationship.

Dwight rested his hand on the small of her back, leading her to where he'd parked his vehicle. He opened the passenger-side door and held her elbow until she was seated. She buckled her seat belt and looked out the windshield as Dwight slipped in behind the wheel rather than have him see her lusting after him.

When she'd opened the door, she was able to take in everything about his appearance in one sweeping glance, committing it to memory: the stark white dress shirt with monogrammed cuff links, charcoal-gray silk tie under the spread collar, tailored suit pants and highly shined imported slip-ons. She could avoid looking at him but there was no way she could dismiss his warmth or the sensual masculine cologne that was the perfect complement to his body's natural pheromones.

Sasha realized she was no different than some of the women in her Nashville social circle whenever they'd gossiped to each other about being horny and wanting to sleep with men other than their husbands. There had come a time when she'd believed some of them had slept with her husband once she moved out of their bedroom. Sasha hadn't missed the sly and surreptitious looks he'd exchanged with one woman, and it wasn't until their divorce was finalized that Sasha's suspicions were confirmed when they were seen coupled up together in public.

Dwight rested his right arm over the back of her seat. "Are you okay, sweetie?"

"Yes."

"You're rather quiet tonight."

"I was just thinking about a few things."

"Do those things have anything to do with *us*?" he asked.

"Some of them."

"Do you want to talk about *them*?"

Sasha knew what she was about to tell Dwight would either bring them closer together or apart. "Do you recall when I told you I didn't want to talk about my ex?"

"I do."

"Well, what I'm about to tell you I've only told one other person."

"Your mother?"

Sasha breathed out an audible sigh as she gathered the strength to reveal to Dwight what she'd sworn never to repeat. She'd told her mother because she had a right to know why she'd come back to Wickham Falls to start up a business, and why she wasn't the same as when she'd returned for the first time in seven years for her father's funeral.

She really didn't want to disclose the circumstances surrounding what people thought of as a fairy-tale marriage between the cowboy and the redhead. But if she hoped to have an uncomplicated relationship with Dwight, then she wanted him to understand her reaction to certain scenarios.

"Yes."

Dwight gave her a quick glance. "Why tell me, Sasha?"

"Because of how I feel about you."

He slowed the Jeep to less than ten miles as he approached the railroad crossing and then, after looking in both directions, drove over the tracks. "And that is?"

Sasha wanted to tell Dwight he wasn't making it easy for her to tell him that she wanted to be more than friends. "I like you, Dwight." Why, she chided, did she sound like an adolescent girl talking to a boy she had a crush on?

He smiled, the dimple creasing his cheek. "That goes for both of us, because I like you, too, Sasha."

"I mean I really like you."

"Are you trying to say you want us to be more than just friends? That we could be friends with benefits?"

The seconds ticked until it became a full minute. *Answer the man*, her inner voice taunted her. "Yes."

Dwight dropped his arm and met her eyes briefly in the glow coming from the dashboard. He wondered what it had taken for her to admit she wanted to engage in a physical relationship. He wasn't immune to Sasha. It was quite the contrary. There were nights when he woke up with an erection and in a cold sweat after he'd dreamed of making love with her. As a virile man in his prime, he'd always had a healthy libido, but since Kiera had come to live with him, he'd elected to remain celibate. He'd never slept with a woman in his home even before becoming a full-time father, preferring instead to entertain women at the lake house. And now that Kiera accompanied him for their fishing outings, even the lake house was off-limits for his clandestine liaisons.

"Do you really believe that I'm that immune to you, Sasha? We're both consenting adults, so sleeping together shouldn't present a problem except that…" His words trailed off.

Sasha placed her hand over his gripping the wheel. "Except that it would complicate everything if we decide to break up," she said, finishing his statement.

"Yes."

"But didn't you say we are adults?"

He nodded. "Yes, I did."

"Then as adults we should not have to resort to child-ish tantrums or play head games where we try to make each other's life miserable because we feel we've been wronged."

"That sounds good."

"You don't believe me, do you?"

Dwight came to a stop at the four-way intersection and waited for traffic to slow enough so he could drive across to the road leading to the Den. "I believe you, sweetie." And he did. Not only did he believe Sasha, but he also appreciated her candor. He'd dealt with women closer to his age than Sasha's and some of them made a habit of being evasive in the belief they were being mysterious, and it was a trait that annoyed him. "And you don't have to tell me about your ex-husband because I've made it a practice not to discuss Kiera's mother with women I go out with."

"Beginning now, talking about exes is prohibited," Sasha said in a quiet voice.

Dwight reversed their hands, his thumb caressing the silken skin and delicate bones on hers. He refused to talk about or bad-mouth Adrienne because he had always respected her as Kiera's mother. His daughter was the best thing to come out of their marriage, and that was something he'd never regretted.

He knew eventually he would be open to listening to Sasha talk about her ex, only because he was aware that she needed to unburden herself to someone other than her mother. However, he didn't want to become a substitute or a catharsis for her to exorcise her ex.

It had taken Dwight years to come to forgive Adrienne for her duplicity. He'd forgiven her for reversing her position to live in The Falls once he'd set up his practice, but what took much longer for him to accept was her admission that she'd slept with another man with whom she had attended college both while they were engaged and during their marriage.

He didn't want to speculate as to why Sasha's marriage hadn't survived the glare of the spotlight as one half of a very public couple. However, he knew what he felt and was beginning to feel about her had nothing to do with her past fame as the go-to pastry chef for celebrities but how she related to him and his family.

Dwight had made up a litany of excuses as to why he couldn't afford to become *that* involved with Sasha and he knew each one rang hollow. He'd told himself that he didn't want to date a woman in the same hometown as his, yet he'd taken Sasha with him to the Den for Military Monday and now she was his date for a local fund-raiser. He'd called her his woman, and to Dwight that meant she was very special—someone he wanted to see exclusively and protect.

He'd conjured up a few roadblocks, the first being she looked nothing like the women he'd dated in the past, but all of them had dissipated like a puff of smoke the first time she came to his home with her mother. Dwight found everything about Sasha refreshing, from her admission that she was just a country girl who'd left the glare of the spotlight in Music City to return to The Falls, and her resolute motivation to make her bakeshop viable.

And then there was Kiera. Any woman he dated had to accept his daughter because they were a package deal, and unknowingly Sasha had passed that test. Kiera tended to dominate their dinner table conversations when she could not stop talking about her boss and the fact that she was seriously thinking of going to culinary school to become a professional chef. When she'd mentioned her intentions to Sasha, the pastry chef told her she would bring her on as an apprentice to teach her the ins and outs of designing cakes. Sasha had also promised Kiera that she could begin giving her lessons in the summer during the days when the shop was closed, which had the teenager so excited she could hardly get the words out coherently.

Dwight was proud of the changes he saw in Kiera. She'd stopped complaining that she had nothing to do because she loved her part-time job at the bakeshop, while she'd managed to maintain her honor student status. Her friendship with the neighbor's daughter now included a few other girls in the neighborhood.

"What if we let things unfold naturally and see where it leads us?"

"I like that," Sasha said, smiling.

Sasha walked into the barn holding on to Dwight's arm over his suit jacket, not seeing the curious looks directed at them when she glanced around the building that was both rustic and ethereal. Strings of tiny white bulbs and gaslight-inspired chandeliers evoked a bygone era. Round tables, with seating for six, were covered with white tablecloths. Colorful Depression glasses and flatware with ornate handles were also in keeping with the designated time period. Her attention was drawn to a mahogany bar, reminiscent of those in old saloons, where several men had gathered to order their favorite libation. She estimated the barn could easily accommodate seventy-five to ninety for a catered event.

The woman checking their names off on a printout smiled up at Dwight. "Dr. Adams, you and your date are assigned to table four."

He returned her smile. "Thank you, Mrs. Nicholls."

"What are you thinking?" Dwight asked in Sasha's ear when they were out of earshot of the woman.

"This is the perfect place to hold a wedding or even prom, without the alcohol, of course."

"I think that's what the Gibsons were thinking about when they put up this place. Aiden said he had a long talk with his uncle about folks having to leave The Falls to have their weddings."

Sasha hadn't been back long enough to know who'd planned their wedding. The exception was Nicole Campos and Fletcher Austen, who'd arranged to host their nuptials at their home. "The Gibsons are very resourceful because they're able to provide the venue, food and alcoholic drinks."

The word *alcohol* was barely off her tongue when a waiter approached with a tray of flutes with a pale bubbly wine. "Champagne, miss?"

She smiled. "Yes, please."

Dwight took the flute from the man and handed it to Sasha before taking one for himself. He touched his glass to hers. "Here's to new beginnings."

"To a new beginning," she repeated in a soft whisper. Sasha took a sip of the wine. It was delicious.

White-jacketed waitstaff circulated with trays of canapés and hors d'oeuvres, while a young woman dressed in chef whites manned a carving station. It was Sasha's first time attending a Wickham Falls soiree, and it was apparent it was on par with some of those she'd attended and catered. Over the years she'd heard people complain that The Falls was stuck in time, but Sasha never felt that way because the residents had always looked out for one another. They came together when someone lost their job or a family member. The church's outreach did their part soliciting donations of food and clothes for the neediest families. And many of the businesses had survived despite the ups and downs of the nation's economy because their motto was: live local, shop local. Members of the town council were aware of their residents' resistance to fast-food and chain stores and consistently voted down their requests to build in The Falls.

Dwight's free arm went around her waist, pulling her closer to his side. "Do you want anything from the carving station?"

Sasha smiled up at him. She was beginning to feel the effects of the champagne. "Yes. I'll come with you."

She spent the remainder of the cocktail hour sampling prawns with an Asian-inspired dipping sauce, filo tartlets with spicy cilantro shrimp, mint-marinated lamb kebabs with a tahini-and-honey dip, and ginger orange pork skewers. Sasha was impressed with the gourmet selections prepared by cooks who were better known for barbecuing, grilling and smoking meat.

Within minutes of Dwight excusing himself to speak to the mayor, Sasha saw Georgina walk in. Her friend was resplendent in a black body-hugging halter dress and her hair tucked into a twist behind her left ear. "You look fabulous," Sasha said, as she and Georgina exchanged air-kisses.

"That goes double for you, Sasha. I love your dress and hair."

"Thanks. Do you always attend this fund-raiser?"

Georgina shook her head. "No. This is my first time. My dad always comes alone, because Mom hates these gatherings. He decided to give me his ticket because he claims it's time I start to represent the business. And before you ask, I still haven't said anything to them about moving out. I want to find a place and sign a lease before I tell them."

Sasha had no intention of offering Georgina any more advice about her family dilemma. After all, blood was thicker than water, and she did not want to be labeled an interloper. "Do you know who you are sitting with?"

"Not yet. I'll be at the table with folks who don't have escorts. By the way, did you come with anyone?" Georgina asked.

Sasha glanced over at her date, who was talking to the mayor and several members of the town council. "Dwight Adams."

Georgina's jaw dropped. "You are dating Dr. Adams?"

She curbed the urge to laugh at Georgina's shocked expression. "Yes. Why do you look so surprised?" It was obvious her friend hadn't heard that she and Dwight were together at the Wolf Den for Military Monday. Sasha did not want to believe her former classmate's life was so insular that she hadn't been aware of the goings-on outside the department store.

"Did you know he's one of The Falls' most eligible bachelors? Of which we have very few," Georgina added. "And he can't seem to take his eyes off you."

Sasha glanced over her shoulder to find Dwight staring at her. A hint of a smile tilted the corners of his mouth and she returned it with one of her own. Overhead light glinted off the silver in his cropped hair, and the contrast between the shimmering strands and his mahogany complexion added to his overall masculine beauty.

She shifted her attention to Georgina, who had a strange look on her face. "What's the matter?"

"You and Dr. Adams, Sasha."

"What about us?"

Georgina was preempted from answering when Langston Cooper joined them. "Good evening, lovely ladies," he drawled, extending a glass filled with an amber liquid in their direction.

"Hello, Langston," Sasha and Georgina chorused in unison.

Langston took a sip of his cocktail, staring at Georgina over the rim of the old-fashioned glass. "I like what the Gibsons have set up here."

"We should've had something like this when we had prom," Sasha said.

"Word," Georgina drawled. "We had the prom from hell when the hotel had a power outage and their generator malfunctioned and everyone started yelling about wanting a refund."

Sasha and Georgina were entertaining Langston with the events following their aborted prom when she detected the fragrance of a familiar men's cologne; she turned to find Dwight standing a short distance away, seemingly waiting before interrupting their animated conversation. Excusing herself, she approached him.

Dwight took her hand, threading their fingers together. "They want us to take our seats because they're going to begin serving dinner."

She saw waiters filling water glasses, while a hostess

was directing guests to their respective tables. Sasha ignored the stares of those following her and Dwight as he escorted her to their table. It was the second time they were seen in public together and she surmised they were curious not only why she had returned to The Falls, but also why Dwight had attended the annual fund-raiser with her rather than his mother.

Dwight pulled out a chair, seated her, and then leaned over and pressed a kiss on her hair. Those sitting at their table, and others nearby, did not miss the tender intimate gesture of affection or Sasha's smile or when she covered the hand resting on her shoulder.

Chapter Eight

Sasha felt the strong, steady beating of Dwight's heart against her breasts as they danced the last dance of the night when the DJ played a slower love song after several upbeat tunes. She'd discovered something else about the man holding her close: he liked to slow dance.

A sumptuous sit-down dinner followed the cocktail hour with dining choices of excellently prepared chicken, grilled bourbon salmon and rib-eye steak. As a chef, Sasha gave the Gibsons a top grade for taste and presentation.

"Did you enjoy your first chamber fund-raiser?" Dwight said, his mouth pressed to her ear.

"Yes. However, they could've done away with the long, windy speeches from the officers of the chamber, otherwise it would've been perfect." The waitstaff had been instructed not to serve the next course until after everyone stopped speaking.

Dwight's arm tightened around her waist as he spun her around and around. "They've been told for years to cut down on the number of speeches, but it looks as if everyone wants their fifteen minutes of fame at the expense of folks enjoying their dinner."

"I still enjoyed it."

"I enjoyed you more."

Sasha did not have a comeback because she believed she'd said too much during the drive over. She didn't want Dwight to see her as a desperate divorcée prowling for her next husband.

Sasha waited until she was seated and belted into the Jeep and Dwight had maneuvered out of the parking area to say, "I want to apologize."

He gave her a sidelong glance. "What for?"

"For being overly aggressive when I told you I wanted more than friendship when you'd already established that wasn't what you wanted."

Dwight stared straight ahead as he concentrated on driving. The silence inside the vehicle swelled to deafening proportions. "There's nothing to apologize for, Sasha. I said what I did because I didn't want you to know that I'd met a woman that had me rethinking the excuses why I didn't want to get involved in a serious relationship. But there was something about you that proved me wrong. I'd promised myself that I would never date another woman from The Falls, and that I couldn't commit to any permanence until Kiera left for college. And more importantly, a woman would have to accept that my daughter comes first in my life."

"And she should be first, Dwight. If I'd had a child,

then my priority would have to be my son or daughter." A beat passed before Sasha asked, "What did I do to make you change your mind?"

He smiled. "Nothing. Just don't change from being that unpretentious redheaded, freckle-faced country girl who makes incredible desserts and prefers going barefoot to wearing shoes."

"So, you like my freckles?"

"Every single one of them. Especially those on your cheeks."

Sasha's bubbly laugh bounced off the roof of the vehicle. "There was a time when I hated my freckles because kids used to tease me saying I had dirt on my face and other epithets referring to flies that I won't repeat."

"Kids can be cruel."

"And they grow up to become cruel adults."

Dwight registered a slight hardness in Sasha's tone, and he wondered if she was referring to her ex-husband. Was the smiling face of the hometown girl splashed across the glossy pages of entertainment magazines all for show? Locals couldn't stop talking about her because she'd married an A-list recording artist and was a celebrity chef to the rich and famous. The showplace mansion she shared with her husband had been featured in many of the popular architectural magazines. She had it all, and then she walked away from it all, refusing to answer reporters' questions. She subsequently disappeared from the public until she returned to where her ancestors had put down roots many generations ago.

He arrived at Sasha's house and walked her to the door, not wanting the night to end although they would see each other the next day for Sunday dinner. Dwight waited for her to unlock and open the door to cradle her face in his hands. Slowly, deliberately, he lowered his head and kissed her until her lips parted under his. He reluctantly ended the kiss. "Good night, sweets."

Sasha smiled. "Good night. And thank you for a wonderful evening."

"Thank you for being the perfect date. I'll see you tomorrow for Sunday dinner."

"Don't forget to bring your appetite."

"I won't."

Dwight waited until Sasha went inside before getting back into the Jeep. He'd wanted to tell Sasha that he was tired of lying—to her and himself. He'd made up so many excuses as to why he didn't want to get involved with her that he hadn't been able to come up with another one. Then there was the excuse that his daughter worked for her, and he didn't want to jeopardize Kiera's future employment if he and Sasha split up. And last was his vow never to date another woman from Wickham Falls.

Dwight felt as if his life was under a microscope the first time Adrienne Wheeler had agreed to go out with him. All the high school boys wanted to date her, and the girls wanted to be her. After they were spotted together at the movies, a collective groan went out through The Falls from guys who'd believed they still had a chance with the flirtatious young coed who'd been blessed with beauty *and* brains.

He recalled the plans they'd made for their futures, both agreeing to becoming engaged before heading off to college. Dwight married Adrienne within days of her college graduation. They'd wanted to wait until after he finished dental school to start a family, but it was as if nature had conspired against them, because despite taking precautions, Adrienne informed him she was pregnant. Becoming parents signaled a change in what had been an uncomplicated passionate relationship. Adrienne complained incessantly that she felt as if she was slowly dying in The Falls and issued veiled hints that it wasn't where she'd wanted to live her entire life like her parents and grandparents before her.

He'd believed he could give Adrienne what she wanted and needed to ensure a happy marriage; however, it wasn't until he saw her with her new husband that he had come to the realization that she truly loved her second husband in a way she could never love her first. Not only did Adrienne appear content with her life, but Dwight was happy for her; he'd made it easy for her to survive her second marriage by assuming full custody of their daughter.

Dwight whistled a nameless tune as he headed home. He'd deliberately avoided encountering Sasha for weeks until she came to his home for Sunday dinner. That encounter changed everything when he'd invited her to accompany him to the Den for Military Monday. He thought of her as a breath of fresh air with her easygoing personality and distinctive high-pitched laugh. What he really liked about her was that what you saw was what you got. There was no pretense or hint that she was anything other than what she'd professed: a country girl down to the marrow in her bones.

Charlotte opened the door and Dwight handed her a large box wrapped in silver paper and black velvet ribbon. "A little something for the house." Pinpoints of red dotted her pale cheeks, and it was obvious Sasha's mother hadn't counted on his bringing anything. "You can't expect us to bring dessert, especially not when Sasha's a pastry chef."

"I heard my name."

Dwight stared over Charlotte's head, his eyes briefly meeting Sasha's. Her transformation was startling from the woman wearing haute couture the night before to one in a seafoam-green surplice, cropped black slacks and matching ballet-type shoes. "I was telling your mother that there's no way we were going to attempt to make dessert and embarrass ourselves."

Charlotte turned and handed Sasha the gift. "Please take this." She peered around Dwight. "Where's Victoria and Kiera?"

"We'd intended to all come together, but they said they had to make a stop. They should be here shortly."

"I'm forgetting my manners. Please come in and rest yourself. As soon as your family gets here, we can sit down to eat. In the meanwhile, can I get you something to drink?"

"No, thanks," Dwight said, as he followed Charlotte into the enclosed front porch and sat on an armchair.

Stretching out his legs, Dwight closed his eyes and crossed his feet at the ankles. A satisfying peace swept over him when he thought about the path his life had taken since his last visit to New York City. He'd loaded up the rental car with Kiera's clothes, while she said her goodbyes to her mother, driving nonstop to Wickham Falls. His daughter was unusually quiet during the trip, and he'd suspected she was experiencing mixed emotions about leaving a city where she'd attended school and spent time with her friends. Kiera, like Adrienne, was a social butterfly, and she literally came alive in the presence of others. He'd suspected the confrontation between his daughter and her stepfather must have been quite volatile if she'd agreed to live with him in a town she referred to as lame with nothing to do.

Dwight had to remind her that she'd learned to drive in The Falls, and once she completed her junior year and passed her driver's test, he would get her a car. His promise had been the deal breaker. He'd taken her out in the Jeep, but Kiera claimed she preferred driving her grandmother's compact.

He'd voiced his concern to Victoria after Kiera was enrolled at the high school when she came home sullen and monosyllabic. Dwight knew she missed her mother, although he doubted whether she would admit it, *and* her friends. And it wasn't until she began working at Sasha's Sweet Shoppe that she'd become more animated, and talked nonstop about how she was able to convince the bakeshop's regular customers to order the day's special, or another pastry they were unfamiliar with.

His cell phone chimed a familiar ringtone, and he removed it from the pocket of his slacks. "Hello, Adrienne."

"Why didn't you tell me my daughter wants to be a cook?"

Dwight rolled his eyes upward. He knew by his ex's strident tone that the conversation was going to be less than friendly. "I didn't have to tell you if she told you."

"She can't be a cook!"

"She wants to be a chef, and that's very different from being a cook."

"I don't need you to tell me the difference, Dwight! You know damn well what I mean."

He sat straight. It wasn't until they were separated

that he had become aware of how argumentative Adrienne could be. It was as if she thrived on being confrontational. "If you're looking for a fight today, then I don't intend to verbally spar with you. Kiera has made up her mind as to what she wants as a career choice, and we agreed a long time ago that I would pay for her college, which lets you off the hook monetarily for any decision she makes."

"I thought she wanted to be a doctor."

"You want her to be a doctor, while I'm open to whatever she chooses to be."

"She told me she wanted to be a doctor until you started sniffing around that Manning girl's skirts."

A muscle twitched in Dwight's jaw when he clenched his teeth. "What did you say?"

"Don't worry, Kiera didn't tell me about you and Sasha Manning because lately she's been like a deaf-mute whenever I ask about you. Although all the Wheelers have left The Falls, I still have a few friends there who keep me up on the latest news."

The Wheelers had begun a steady exodus over the decades from Wickham Falls, until even Kiera's distant cousins were gone. "If you're so concerned about what's going on here, then you should've never left. Goodbye," Dwight said, abruptly ending the call. He knew if it hadn't been for Kiera, he would've cut off all communication with Adrienne. He was aware she was upset because their daughter had refused to give her any information on his private life, which had him totally confused when her focus should've been on her husband. The few encounters he'd had with the man over the years had been congenial once Dwight set the ground rules for how he wanted him, as a stepfather, to relate to Kiera. He'd been forthcoming when he warned Omar Johnson never to lay a hand on Kiera or there would be hell to pay.

At the time, Dwight didn't know what had transpired between Omar and Kiera until she finally told him that she'd overheard her stepfather tell someone he hated his wife's daughter and he couldn't wait to get rid of her, yet knew there was no way Dwight would go along with Adrienne sending their daughter to boarding school to save her marriage, because it had been apparent that Kiera wasn't the most important person in her life.

Generally, he ignored Adrienne and didn't let her get under his skin, but today was different, because it involved Sasha. And because Kiera refused to talk to her mother about him, Adrienne had contacted locals who'd told her what she wanted to know about his personal life. What he had never been able to wrap his head around was Adrienne's desire to know about the women he dated when she had recently celebrated her twelfth wedding anniversary with a man who obviously adored her.

Dwight detected movement out of the side of his eye and stood up. Sasha had come into the room without making a sound. "How much did you hear?" he asked her, not knowing how long she had been standing there.

Sasha saw Dwight's thunderous expression and wondered what had set him off. "What are you talking about?"

"Were you eavesdropping on my telephone conversation?"

"No!" The single word exploded from her mouth, as she struggled to control her temper. "And I don't appreciate you implying that I'm a sneak."

Dwight ran a hand over his face and then took a step and cradled her against his chest. "I'm sorry, babe. I had no right to take out my frustrations on you."

Wrapping her arms around his waist, Sasha leaned back and looked up at him. "I'll forgive you this time but try not to let it happen again." Her words, though spoken quietly, held a thread of hardness that indicated she was serious. She'd experienced enough of Grant taking his frustrations out on her to last her a lifetime. He'd expected every song he released to reach number one on the country chart. As the ultimate narcissist, he thought earning the number two spot made him a loser.

Dwight brushed his mouth over hers. "I promise, it won't happen again."

Her annoyance vanished with his promise and chaste kiss. "I came to get you because I need you to be my taste tester."

"Can you give me a hint what I'll be eating?"

"You won't be eating but drinking. I've been experimenting with mocktails. I have dozens of photos of cakes, along with signed releases from former celebrity clients, filed away because I plan to publish a coffee-table book featuring desserts and accompanying drinks."

Sasha looped her arm through Dwight's and led him through the living and dining rooms, where warming dishes lined a buffet table. Her mother had decided to serve a buffet dinner in lieu of a sit-down because the dining room table, unlike the Adamses', wasn't large enough to accommodate the dishes she'd prepared for her guests.

"Something really smells good," Dwight remarked.

Sasha smiled. "My mother is an incredible cook."

"Is she the reason you went to culinary school?"

"Yes and no. I'll tell you about that at another time."

Charlotte glanced up from slicing ingredients for a mixed citrus salad. "I suppose Natasha wants you to…" Her words trailed off when the doorbell chimed throughout the house. She set down a knife. "You kids stay here. I'll get the door."

Sasha rested her hand on Dwight's back, feeling the warmth of his body through his shirt. "I can't remember the last time I've seen my mother this excited to have company. Now that my brothers aren't stationed stateside, she doesn't get to see her grandchildren as much as she would like."

"Where are they stationed?" Dwight asked.

"Philip lives in Germany and Stephen was recently transferred to Guam."

"Has she been putting pressure on you to give her a grandchild that lives closer to home?"

She didn't want to tell Dwight that when she was married her mother had asked her constantly when she was going to have a baby, and she'd told Charlotte she wasn't ready to start a family, that she'd had plenty of time before her biological clock began winding down. And she still had time. At thirty-two, she estimated she had at least three or even four years before being considered high risk, although women were having their first child well into their forties.

"No," Sasha replied. "Mama knows this is not the right time for me to have a baby." She picked up a martini glass with tiny purple flower petals floating atop pale green sparkling liquid and handed it to Dwight. "I want and need your honest opinion," she said, as Dwight put the glass to his mouth. Sasha hadn't realized she'd been holding her breath until she felt a band of tightness constrict her chest. "What? What?" she repeated after he'd taken a deep swallow.

Instead of answering Sasha, Dwight drained the glass. "It's delicious. How did you make it?"

Sasha's smile was dazzling. "You really like it?"

"I did say it was delicious. So yes, I really, really like it."

"What did you taste, Dwight?"

"Lime, a hint of mint, tonic water and something sweet to offset the acidity of the citrus."

"It's lavender. I use it in cakes and frostings."

Dwight set the glass on the countertop. "I never would've guessed that."

"What wouldn't you have guessed?"

Sasha turned to find Victoria and Kiera smiling at them. Kiera cradled a bouquet of fresh roses in every conceivable hue nestled in baby's breath, and wrapped in cellophane, while Victoria held a shopping bag. "Oh, my word. The roses are beautiful."

"Grammie had to drive to Mineral Springs to get them, because the florist here didn't get his shipment of flowers for the week," Kiera volunteered.

Victoria handed Sasha the bag. "This is a little something for the house."

Sasha unwrapped the box and opened it to find an exquisite Waterford vase. It was more than a little something, but to refuse the gift would demonstrate ungratefulness. Folks in the South were raised never to come to someone's home empty-handed.

"Thank you. Mama and I really appreciate your generous gift."

Victoria waved her hand. "I should be the one thanking you for spoiling us when Kiera comes home every night with dessert." She spied the martini glasses and a pitcher filled with the fizzy green liquid. "That really looks exotic."

"It's a take on a green dragon without the alcohol. I wanted to make something Kiera can also drink."

Kiera, who'd busied herself removing the cellophane from the flowers and arranging them in the vase, glanced over her shoulder. "Daddy told me he would disown me if I was caught drinking before I reach the legal age."

"That would be one time when I would side with your father," Victoria said, as she gave her granddaughter a long, penetrating stare.

Kiera lowered her eyes and went back to concentrating on the floral arrangement, and Sasha knew the young girl probably counted on her grandmother as an ally to support her when she wanted something from Dwight. But apparently underage drinking was an issue that was not debatable.

Charlotte removed her apron and picked up the bowl with the salad. "Now that everyone's here, we can go into the dining room to eat. Tonight's menu celebrates the Big Easy with dishes I learned from my grandmother who grew up in New Orleans before she married Granddaddy and moved to The Falls."

Dwight waited until everyone had served themselves before he picked up a bowl and filled it with chicken-andouille gumbo and topped the steaming soup with long-grain cooked rice. He knew from the first spoonful where Sasha had inherited her cooking skills. He ate sparingly because he wanted to sample every dish:

shrimp étouffée, red beans and rice, stuffed pork chops with creole seasoning and jalapeño corn bread. Sasha's mocktail was the perfect complement to offset the incredibly delicious rich and spicy dishes. And he'd discovered he wasn't the only one going back for second helpings.

Everything was perfect from the floral arrangement in the crystal vase, to the delicious iciness of the virgin cocktail, prepared food and the company. It was the second time the Mannings and Adamses had gathered for Sunday dinner, and for Dwight, it felt as if they were truly family. Conversations segued from world and national politics to professional sports teams' playoffs and championship games, and the upcoming events at Kiera's school. She revealed she'd joined a committee to plan events for the following year's graduation. She said students in the junior class were currently involved in planning car washes and bowling fund-raisers to offset the cost of their senior trip.

"Has the committee decided where they want to go for their senior trip?" Sasha asked Kiera.

"The choices are New York, Philadelphia and DC. Someone mentioned taking a three- or four-day cruise, but most kids said their parents can't afford prom and a cruise."

"That is a lot of financial responsibility for parents," Dwight admitted. It wouldn't be a hardship for him to pay for prom and a cruise, but he couldn't say the same for families that weren't as affluent as his.

"This is when some of the civic organizations ought to step up and support our kids," Victoria said. "Dwight, I'm certain the chamber takes in enough with dues and their various fund-raisers throughout the year to at least underwrite the cost of prom, which would provide some monetary relief for parents paying for the senior trip."

"The Gibsons' donation to prom could be their new catering venue, which would put quite a dent in the cost of the tickets," Sasha added. She saw four pairs of eyes staring at her. "Did I say something wrong?"

"No, you didn't," Victoria replied. "In fact, that's a wonderful idea. It's about time the businesses in The Falls support our kids expressly when they want us to shop locally."

"Which we definitely do," Charlotte said in agreement. "I can't remember the last time I went to Mineral Springs or even Beckley for something I could get here."

Victoria touched her napkin to her mouth. "That does it. Charlotte, when you have some spare time I want you to help me get some of the ladies together. We need to spearhead a campaign to help our graduating seniors defray some of the cost of prom and their senior trip. Of course, it's too late for this graduating class, so it would have to be for next year."

Dwight leaned back in his chair, winking at Charlotte. "I want to warn you that my mother is as tenacious as a pit bull once she gets the proverbial bee in her bonnet. She will not stop until she forces someone to submit to her will."

Charlotte smiled. "If that's the case, then she has a sister in crime, because I don't believe in giving up easily." She suddenly sobered. "Being married to a man who couldn't stop beating his gums because everything had to be his way, or no way, prepared me to go the distance."

Rising slightly, Victoria reached across the table and

exchanged a fist bump with Charlotte. "We're going to make an awesome team."

"Grammie, I hope you won't embarrass me," Kiera said.

Dwight looked at his daughter and then his mother. "Did I miss something?"

Victoria lowered her eyes. "No comment."

His eyebrows rose questioningly when his gaze returned to Kiera, who appeared more interested in the food on her plate. "You don't have to tell me. But remember, what doesn't come out in the wash will always come out in the rinse." Dwight knew his mother was his daughter's secret keeper, and he'd come to respect their close bond. However, he trusted Victoria to come to him if she felt a situation would negatively impact her granddaughter.

"And keeping with the theme of the Big Easy, I decided to make bananas Foster for dessert," Sasha said, shattering the uncomfortable silence.

Kiera jumped. "Can I help you make it, Miss Sasha?"

Pushing back her chair, Sasha stood. "Of course."

Dwight rose to his feet. "Mom, you and Miss Charlotte relax while I put away the leftovers."

"Are you sure?" the two older women said in unison.

"Yes, I am sure."

"Natasha will show you where I keep the containers to store the leftovers."

Dwight smiled at Sasha's mother. "Yes, ma'am." Stacking plates and flatware, he carried them into the kitchen, setting them on the countertop. He glanced at Sasha and Kiera as they peeled and sliced bananas, and the single act of shared domesticity rendered him motionless for several seconds. In that instant he realized he'd never witnessed Kiera and Adrienne together in their kitchen. Whenever he went to New York to see his daughter, he always checked into a hotel and met her in the lobby of the high-rise building where she lived with her mother and stepfather. Even when he'd sat down with Adrienne and Omar to discuss Kiera's future, the meeting took place in a restaurant.

Dwight was certain Adrienne loved her daughter, and Kiera her mother, and while he'd accepted some blame that she wasn't able to grow up with mother and father living under the same roof, he'd trusted Adrienne to protect and raise their daughter properly and she had. Not only was Kiera a good student but she appeared to be well-adjusted.

He'd stored the food in the refrigerator and stacked dishes in the dishwasher when Sasha announced she was ready to serve dessert. Sasha ignited the pan with light brown sugar, melted butter, bananas, cinnamon and dark rum. He watched as she carefully spooned the sauce over the bananas until the flame burned out and immediately ladled it over scoops of vanilla ice cream. It was only the second time Dwight had eaten the dessert, but the former could not come close to what Sasha had prepared.

"Did you buy the ice cream from the Village Market?" Victoria asked Sasha. "Because this brand is delicious."

Dwight wanted to ask the same thing. The Falls' supermarket, although smaller than many of the area's supermarkets and warehouse stores, was stocked with everything the residents needed to stock their refrigerators and pantries.

"Natasha makes her own ice cream," Charlotte said,

smiling. "I love her vanilla because she uses the actual beans, but her pistachio is to die for."

Victoria set down her spoon. "Sasha, I know I'm not giving you a lot of notice, but can you make an assortment of desserts for my Ladies Auxiliary meeting this coming Wednesday? Although many of us don't need the extra calories, I'd like you to make enough ice cream to serve eight."

Dwight met her eyes across the table, and he wondered if she was feeling that his mother had put her on the spot. He was aware that she worked long hours to grow her business and she'd mentioned she was looking to take on an assistant, which would free her up to accept special orders.

"I can put together a tray of miniature desserts along with a couple of pints of gelato, which has a lot less butterfat than ice cream."

"We don't have classes on Wednesday, because teachers have professional development on that day," Kiera said excitedly. "Can I come in and help you, Miss Sasha?"

"I don't mind, but you'll have to ask your father."

"Daddy, pul-eeze," Kiera drawled. "Can I?"

His daughter gave a longing look she knew he could not resist. "Yes."

Kiera jumped up, rounded the table, wrapped her arms around his neck and kissed his cheek. "Thank you, Daddy."

He held on to her hands. "You're welcome, baby girl."

Kiera pressed her mouth to his ear. "I'm too old to be your baby girl," she whispered.

"When I'm in my nineties and you're seventy you will still be my baby girl."

"Stop it, Daddy. You're embarrassing me."

Dwight kissed the back of her hand and then removed her arms from around his neck. What his daughter failed to understand was that he'd missed so many years watching her grow up to become the young woman she now presented. Visiting with her three or four times a year wasn't the same as seeing the milestones in which she went from a toddler to an adolescent, and he'd had to rely on Adrienne to tell him about the physical changes in their daughter's body.

He had less than two years before losing her again when she attended college. By that time, she would probably have a boyfriend who would become the most significant man in her life. Dwight hoped, if or when she married, she would find a partner who would love and, more important, respect her. Sasha shared a smile with Kiera when she retook her seat beside her.

He didn't know if it was a passing fancy that Kiera wanted to become a chef because the baking bug had hit from working in the bakeshop, but if it wasn't then he intended to support her totally until she achieved her goal.

Chapter Nine

Dwight parked behind a pickup along the street opposite Fletcher Austen's house, where Fletcher was scheduled to exchange vows with Nicole Campos. He hadn't
planned to stay long because he wanted to drive to the
lake house later that night to stock it with provisions
he would need for the coming months. He'd bought the
property on a whim when one of his patients had left
the prospectus in the office waiting room. A developer
was putting up one- and two-bedroom homes in a gated
community around a lake with picturesque views of
tree-covered mountains, thick forested areas and twin
waterfalls that flowed into the lake. All the properties
had docks for boat owners who were able to store them
on the premises during the winter season.

Dwight knew he didn't need another house, but once
he closed on the property, he'd contemplated that it

would be the perfect place to vacation and possibly live once he retired. However, retirement was still a long time away, and as a single father of a teenage daughter, his plans were on hold until Kiera was emancipated. He'd asked Kiera if she wanted to join him at the lake house for the weekend, but she declined because she had to finish reading *A Tale of Two Cities*, and write an essay on what Dickens was attempting to convey about the social and economic conditions of England during the time he'd written the novel. She'd complained because she was taking French as a foreign language and preferred reading about authors who wrote about French history.

Dwight saw the familiar white van that belonged to Sasha's Sweet Shoppe parked in the driveway. He smiled when he saw her coming out of the house. She wore her usual white tunic with the shop's name stitched over her heart and a pair of black-and-white-striped chef's slacks. Her recognizable red hair was concealed under a white bandanna.

"Fancy meeting you here," he teased.

"I just delivered the wedding cake."

His eyebrows rose slightly. "Are you coming back for the ceremony and reception?" he asked.

"No. I'm going home to put my feet up and do nothing more strenuous than inhale and exhale. I've been going nonstop all week."

"Why don't you hang out with me this weekend?" The invitation had rolled off Dwight's tongue so quickly that it had shocked him.

Sasha blinked slowly. "Where?"

He successfully bit back a smile when he realized she hadn't said no. "At my lake house. I'm going up there later tonight and plan to stay over until Monday night."

"Don't you have office hours on Monday?"

This time Dwight did smile. It was apparent she had remembered his office hours. "Not again until after Labor Day. Once I start spending time at the lake, I take off Saturday through Monday."

"It's nice when you can make your own hours."

"You can make your own hours, Sasha. You talk about going home and vegging out for the next few days because you're working too hard. What you must do is work smart. I've been where you are now. I tried running a practice with serving one weekend a month and another two weeks in the summer, plus going to New York several times a year to spend time with Kiera. It affected me mentally and physically."

"What did you do?"

"I restructured office hours and added a dental assistant to the existing staff. And now that I'm civilian and I have sole custody of Kiera, I've restructured my life."

Sasha angled her head, seemingly deep in thought. "Other than hire an assistant, how do you suggest I restructure my life?"

"Come with me to the lake house tonight. You won't have to do anything more strenuous than lifting a fork to eat."

She smiled. "Do you plan to go fishing?"

"Not this weekend. I went shopping to stock the pantry and the fridge, so the first order of business will be getting the place ready for the season."

"It sounds tempting."

"Look, Sasha, I don't want to put any pressure on you. I'm going to be here for a couple of hours. If you decide you want to join me, then send me a text and I'll swing by and pick you up." He lowered his head and kissed her forehead. "Take care of yourself, sweetie."

Dwight waited for Sasha to get into the van and back out of the driveway before he walked around the house to the back, where a tent had been erected to accommodate the guests who'd come to witness the wedding of a couple who'd grown up in Wickham Falls. Fletcher had joined the army and Nicole the Corps following their high school graduation. They'd recently reunited when Nicole moved back to The Falls to take care of her nephews while their father was treated for an opioid addiction stemming from the injuries he sustained in an automobile accident that had claimed the life of his wife and their unborn child.

Dwight and Reggie Campos were best friends in high school, and he had volunteered to be his sponsor, but instead of returning to The Falls to live, the former college assistant defensive football coach had elected to live in Florida, where he had undergone treatment in a private residential facility. When Fletcher had come by to give Dwight the invitation, he'd informed him that Nicole's brother, parents and nephews were coming to The Falls for the wedding, and Dwight was looking forward to reuniting with his old friend.

The invitation indicated casual attire, and in lieu of gifts the bride and groom had requested their guests make online donations to the Wounded Warrior Project. Both had completed several tours of duty. Nicole had piloted Black Hawk helicopter gunships. Fletcher was a Special Forces medical sergeant, whose career ended when shrapnel from a rocket-propelled grenade tore through his right leg, shattering bone and damaging muscle.

It became Military Monday on steroids as Dwight greeted and was greeted by the crowd of predominantly military people gathering under the tent from which came mouthwatering aromas of smoking and grilling meat. Chairs were set up theater-style in a clearing beyond the tent where the ceremony was scheduled to take place. It was the perfect afternoon for a wedding with midday temperatures in the low seventies and there wasn't a cloud in the bright blue sky.

Dwight applauded Fletcher and Nicole for hosting an informal barbecue wedding reception in their backyard rather than in the ballroom of a hotel. He recalled his own wedding, which quickly turned from a small intimate affair into something close to a televised celebrity production. Adrienne's parents were willing to jump through hoops to give their only daughter whatever she wanted, even if it meant withdrawing money from their retirement nest egg.

A wide smile split Dwight's face when he spied Reggie coming out of the house. His friend wasn't as thin as he'd been before leaving The Falls and there were flecks of gray in his cropped hair that weren't apparent during their last encounter, but he had to admit Reggie looked much healthier.

"Hey, buddy," he said, wrapping Reggie in a bear hug.

Reggie pounded Dwight's back. "Man, it's good to see you. I just got in last night and the first thing I asked Nikki was if she'd invited you."

"Even if she hadn't, I still would've crashed this get-together if only to see you." He held his friend at arm's length. His tawny-brown complexion was deeply tanned. "You look good, Reggie."

"I feel good, Dwight. I must admit that getting and staying clean is a daily struggle. But whenever I look at my boys, I know I can't go down that rabbit hole again. Nikki sacrificed too much for me to start using again."

"Your sister is an exceptional woman."

"That she is," Reggie said in agreement.

"How long are you going to hang out in The Falls?" Dwight asked him.

"We're just going to be here overnight. I have a job interview Monday morning to coach football at a Dade County high school. Even though I prefer coaching on a college level, I'll take what I can get to get back into the game."

"You have my number. Contact me once you get settled into a routine, and maybe we can get together to catch up on old times."

"I'd like that, Dwight. I just bought a three-bedroom condo overlooking the ocean, so I'm adjusting to opening my door and not walking out on grass, while the boys are adjusting well to their new school."

Dwight chatted with Reggie for a few more minutes until someone told Reggie he was needed inside. He thought about what his friend had said about how difficult it was for him to maintain sobriety. Reggie had been one of a growing number of people who began taking prescription pain meds and after a while found themselves addicted to the substances. At first members of the town council were in denial when they claimed Wickham Falls did not have a drug problem, but with a rising crime rate attributed to substance abuse, they were forced to act by agreeing to open and support a substance abuse clinic. Dwight no longer wrote out prescriptions but faxed them directly to the pharmacist to be filled. The pharmacy was installed with cameras and a silent alarm that went directly to the sheriff's office.

The wedding went off smoothly with an exchange of vows and rings, and it was followed by a buffet reception with tables groaning with food. A DJ spun upbeat tunes that had most gyrating to the music as they ate, drank and shouted to one another to be heard above the din. Dwight checked his watch after Nicole cut the cake and slices of each layer were handed out to the guests, and decided to leave because he wanted to reach the lake before it was completely dark. The three exquisitely decorated cakes were artistic masterpieces with the detail Sasha had lavished on the roses and leaves. He had no idea of how long it had taken her to decorate the cakes, but now he knew why she'd admitted to having gone nonstop all week.

He slipped away without saying anything to the newly married couple, who were dancing to a slow tune, and got into his vehicle. Reaching into the glove box, he retrieved his cell phone. He had one text message.

Natasha: I'm ready whenever you are.

Dwight smothered a laugh. It looked as if he was going to have a houseguest for the weekend.

Dwight: I'll pick you up at 8.

Sasha knocked softly on the door to her mother's bedroom to get her attention. Charlotte sat in her favorite chair, feet resting on the matching footstool, as she watched a James Bond movie she had seen several times.

"Mama, I just wanted to tell you that I'm going to be away for a couple of days."

Charlotte sat straight. "Where are you going?"

"Dwight invited me to spend the weekend at his lake house."

Charlotte's blue eyes grew wider, and then she smiled. "Good for you. Enjoy yourself."

"I'll try, Mama."

"Don't try, Natasha. Just do it."

She would have had to be completely dense not to figure out that Charlotte wanted her and Dwight together. Well, they were together, but as friends. They'd talked about letting everything unfold naturally, and that was what she intended to do.

She'd packed a bag with enough clothes to last her several days and was waiting on the porch when Dwight drove up. Sasha was off the porch before he came to a complete stop and walked around to the passenger side, going completely still when she realized he was the only one in the vehicle.

Sasha opened the rear door and placed her bag on the seat, and then got in next to Dwight. "Where's Kiera?"

Leaning to his right, Dwight pressed a kiss on her hair. "She has to complete a paper for Monday."

"So, it's just us?" she asked.

"You and me, babe. Do you think you'll be able to put up with me for a couple of days?"

"That can go both ways, Dwight. Do you think you can tolerate me for more than a few hours?"

"We'll see, won't we? Buckle up, sweetie."

Sasha fastened her seat belt. "How long will it take to get there?"

"About twenty minutes." Dwight shifted into Reverse and backed out of the driveway. "Why don't you take a nap? I'll wake you when we arrive."

"That's okay. I took a nap after I left Fletcher's place. By the way, how was the wedding?"

"Very nice. The ceremony went off without a hitch with Fletcher and Nikki writing their own vows. Everyone was raving about the scrumptious cake, so be prepared for your phone to ring off the hook because folks were talking about ordering from you."

Sasha exhaled an audible sigh of relief. She hadn't lost her touch. For her, cakes had to be more than pretty; they also had to taste good. "I need an assistant ASAP."

"Have you advertised for one?"

"Yes. I've contacted several cooking schools in and out of the state for a qualified candidate. At this point I'm so desperate that I'm willing to pay more than the entry-level salary for a new graduate."

"Have you had to turn away any orders?"

"One." Sasha told Dwight about a woman who'd decided to give her sister a surprise birthday party and wanted a specialized cake the following day. "I would've made the cake if I hadn't been committed to baking four hundred cupcakes for the Johnson County Schools' PTA bake sale."

Dwight whistled under his breath. "How long did it take you to make them?"

"It took me four hours to bake the cupcakes, and another two to frost and decorate."

"How much advance time did you get for the cupcakes?"

Sasha turned her head, staring out the side window. "Two days. I know they didn't give me much time, but I make allowances for nonprofits."

"Well, for the next two days you can put aside your whisk and pastry bag to decompress."

"I'm looking forward to it."

Sasha was anticipating a quiet, relaxed weekend with a gentle, compassionate man who made her believe in love. When she'd admitted to Grant that she loved him enough to become his wife, she'd believed they would spend the rest of their lives together. However, her fairy-tale world dissipated like a puff of smoke within days of their honeymoon when her new husband turned into someone she didn't recognize. When she questioned his mood swings, he dismissed it with the excuse that he tended to be temperamental when working on new music. She shook her head to banish all thoughts of her ex-husband. He was her past and she wanted him to remain in the past—even in her memory.

The sun had set, and it was difficult to discern the passing landscape as Dwight increased his speed. Stars dotted the darkening sky like minute particles of diamond dust on black velvet, and a near-full moon reminded Sasha of a wheel of creamy white cheese. Sinking lower in the seat, she pressed her head against the headrest as a gentle peace settled over her.

The trees lining the narrow road were taller and seemingly closer together until there was pitch-blackness if not for the Jeep's headlights. The hoot of an owl could be heard through the open windows along with the sounds of other nocturnal wildlife. Dwight shifted into a lower gear as the road seemed to rise out of nowhere, her ears popping with the higher elevation. A sprinkling of lights appeared in the distance and less than a minute later she saw lights reflecting off a large lake from houses ringing the water like a wreath. There were a few boats moored to docks leading from the homes to the water. A posted sign indicated all visitors must stop at the gatehouse.

Dwight's lake house was in a private gated community seemingly in the middle of nowhere.

"Do you own a boat?"

Dwight gave her a quick glance. "No, because I wouldn't get much use out of it." He tapped a remote device attached to the vehicle's visor, the gate went up and he drove through.

"What made you decide to buy property here?" Sasha questioned.

"I found it by accident."

She listened intently when he told her about finding the prospectus left by a patient in the waiting room that piqued his curiosity. The developer's original plan was for a retirement community, but the first couple of years he could only sell two of the dozen houses set on half-acre lots. Once he lowered the fifty-five and older age requirement and dropped the selling price, buyers were more receptive.

"I'm glad I bought in early because the value of the homes has nearly doubled."

"Do you plan to retire here?" She'd asked Dwight a lot of questions, but Sasha wanted to know more about the man with whom she would share a roof for two nights.

Dwight maneuvered along an unpaved road with LED pathway lights. "I'm still undecided. When I retire, I'm not certain whether I'll keep the house in The Falls, but if I do decide to continue to live there, then I'll give this place to Kiera to use it as a vacation property—but that all depends on whether she chooses to live in the state. After all, she is a city girl."

Sasha smiled. Kiera was a city girl who'd come to the country, and she was a country girl who'd left to go to the city. But she'd come back, and there hadn't been one day since her return that she regretted leaving a place she'd called home for almost half her life. She fled Wickham Falls at eighteen and returned fourteen years later at thirty-two and knowingly a lot more mature and hopefully wiser.

She was resolute when it came to her career, but still the proverbial babe in the woods when it came to her heart. Sasha had learned quite a bit about herself in fourteen years and that she had to stop letting her heart rule her head. Here she was with a man who had and was everything she wanted in a lover or husband and he continued to relate to her as if they were besties. It hadn't mattered that they'd shared a few kisses—chaste ones at that. She wanted more, and the more was the need to be desired.

Sasha didn't need to lie on a therapist's couch to bare her soul to get the answers to questions that had nagged at her for years. As the only girl in the family, she wanted her father to dote on her the way she saw Dwight act with Kiera. Even as a single part-time father, Dwight had exhibited more affection toward his daughter than her father had ever shown her in eighteen years. It was only after she'd ended her relationship with the cooking school instructor that she had come to the realization that she saw him as a father figure, someone to love and protect her.

She did not need a man to take care of her financially—that she could do for herself. What she craved was his being there for her when what she'd planned failed, while encouraging her to try it again or suggesting an alternative. She wanted to be able to pour out her heart and have him listen even if he didn't have the answers she needed.

"This is us," Dwight said, breaking into her tortured musings. "Wait here for me while I check inside."

Staring out the windshield, she saw a house that reminded her of pictures of chalets. Twin lanterns flanking the front door provided enough light for her to see the tall window over the loft area Dwight had mentioned. She got out and retrieved her weekender as Dwight walked up the path and opened the front door. Light illuminated the entire first story. He disappeared for several minutes, and when he reappeared in the doorway he beckoned her to come in.

Sasha's jaw dropped when she walked into the yawning space with high ceilings. French doors at the rear of the house offered views of the lake that appeared a great deal farther away than she'd originally thought. The interior was spotless with gleaming wood floors, and the faint aroma of lemon still lingered in the air. She jumped slightly when Dwight reached for her free hand.

"Come with me. I'll show you your bedroom and the bathroom. I have an en suite bath in mine, so that eliminates sharing one."

"Where's your bedroom?"

"It's at the other side of the house. The bath and bedrooms are the only rooms in the house with doors. The kitchen, dining area and the living rooms share an open floor plan. After you get up tomorrow morning, I'll give you a tour of the loft and the backyard. There's a path in the back that leads directly to the lake."

"How much land do you have here?"

"Each house is set on a half acre, which does provide us some privacy from our closest neighbors."

Sasha noticed it was the second time he'd referred to them as *us*. He touched a switch on the wall outside the bedroom and light flooded the space with full-size and twin beds. The vibrant colors of pink, red and lavender in a woven rug were repeated in the bedcovers, and pillow shams provided a radiant contrast to the bleached pine furniture. Floor-to-ceiling off-white lined drapery covered a wall of windows.

"This is very nice. I'm really going to enjoy sleeping here."

"The bathroom has everything you need, but if you're missing something, then let me know and I'll drive into town and pick it up for you."

Sasha turned and smiled up at Dwight as he stared down at her under lowered lids. What was going on behind those dark orbs? she wondered. Then another thought popped into her head. How many women, other than his mother and daughter, had he brought to the house on the lake? Had he bought this place to use as a rendezvous for his liaisons? After all, Dwight appeared to be a very virile man who did not lack for female attention. She'd noticed women staring at him whenever they were together, and first she thought they were curious, but after a while she noticed a coquettish smile, or a slight touch of their hair, and some were even bold enough to wink at him, all of which he tended to ignore.

"I'm good, Dwight. I brought everything I need with me."

"Good night. And try to sleep in as late as you want."

"Okay. Good night."

Sasha waited for him to leave before she closed the door. She'd showered and brushed her teeth before he came to pick her up, so all she needed was to get a nightgown out of her bag, put it on and crawl into bed. Three minutes later, she did just that, and within seconds of her head touching the pillow she was sound asleep.

It took Dwight three trips to unload the provisions he'd stored in the Jeep's cargo area. A large cooler was filled with perishables he stored in the refrigerator/freezer, and crates of dry and canned goods lined the shelves in a pantry tucked into an alcove of the kitchen.

He'd come to the house on Wednesday to remove dustcovers from the furniture, open windows to let out the mustiness, put clean linen on the beds, clean bathrooms, and dust floors and hard surfaces. This year he'd opened two weeks later than he normally would have now that Kiera was living with him. Becoming a full-time father forced him to rearrange his life where he no longer had to think only of himself and his mother, but also his child. He'd resigned his commission in the military, hadn't slept with a woman since he brought Kiera back from New York, and he had curtailed his visits to the lake because Kiera complained about the isolation. If she found Wickham Falls boring, then staying at the lake house was so mind-numbing that she felt more dead than alive.

He'd asked himself over and over what he was doing bringing Sasha to the place he thought of as his private retreat where he openly entertained women when it hadn't been possible in Wickham Falls. The town was too small, the residents too curious, and gossip that spread like a lighted fuse attached to a stick of dynamite made it impossible for him to date a local woman. That was before Natasha Manning came back to town. Not only were they seen together at social functions, but now he had invited her to a place no one, other than his mother and daughter, knew about.

And as much as he'd found himself attracted to Sasha, and wanted to sleep with her, Dwight knew that wasn't going to happen this weekend. He hadn't missed the dark bluish circles under her eyes or her slowed movements indicating she was close to complete exhaustion. He'd invited her to the lake for her and himself. Here she could do absolutely nothing more strenuous than sleep and/or sit and stare at the water. He'd planned to cook, watch a few old movies and while away the hours until it was time to return to The Falls.

Dwight retreated to his bedroom, closed the door, stripped naked and walked into the bathroom to shower and brush his teeth. Tomorrow was a new day and he looked forward to spending it with a woman who'd managed to slip under the armor he wore to protect himself from future heartbreak. He'd fallen in love with Adrienne, and despite their breakup and divorce, a part of him still loved her. And she knew that.

He'd tried exorcising her with other women but failed miserably. Dwight wasn't certain whether he was to blame or if it was because of Kiera that he still felt a connection with Adrienne. After all, they did share a child. What he found puzzling was why she hadn't had more children with Omar.

Turning off the water, he stepped out of the shower stall and dried his body. Walking on bare feet, he made his way into the bedroom and got into bed—alone. His last thoughts weren't of his ex-wife, but Sasha. Whenever she looked up at him through her lashes, the seductive gesture was nearly his undoing. His body silently taunted him over his self-induced celibacy.

Let everything unfold naturally. The very words he'd said to her flooded his mind as he adjusted the pillows under his head. One thing Dwight knew for certain. Once they made love there would be no turning back.

Chapter Ten

Sasha woke, totally disoriented. She'd lost track of place and time. Sitting up, she saw light coming through the drawn drapes and was suddenly aware of where she was. Her cell phone was still in the weekender, so she couldn't discern whether it was early morning or the afternoon. Swinging her legs over the side of the bed, she retrieved her cell phone. It was after ten in the morning. She hadn't slept that late since opening the shop. She scooped up the toiletry bag and walked out of the bedroom to the bath.

Peering into the mirror over the twin sinks, she studied her face. The puffiness under her eyes was gone but not the dark circles. She'd grown up angry because she'd inherited her mother's fair coloring, while her brothers had their father's dark hair, eyes and ruddy complexion.

Any other time she would have attempted to hide

the circles with concealers, but not today. What Dwight saw was what he was going to get—the unadulterated, freckles-and-all Natasha Manning. She decided to take a bath instead of a shower and it felt good just to relax in the tub until the water cooled and forced her to get out. Wrapping a towel around her body, she went back into the bedroom and closed the door.

She found Dwight sitting at a table on the patio at the rear of the house drinking coffee. He'd propped his bare feet on another chair, and she wondered why he hadn't chosen one of four chaises on which to relax.

She slid back the screen and stepped out into the brilliant morning sunlight.

"Good morning."

Setting down the mug, he came to his feet. Sasha swallowed an inaudible gasp as she stared at the magnificence of his tall, lean, muscular body in a black tank top and khaki walking shorts. It was the first time she'd seen him bare that much skin and it shocked her senses. How was she going to maintain a modicum of control when he blatantly put his body on display like that? He hadn't shaved and the emerging stubble only enhanced his magnetism.

Dwight approached her and cradled her face between his hands. "Good morning." Lowering his head, he brushed his mouth over hers. "You look pretty and well rested." She had selected to wear a pale pink crinkle-cotton seersucker sleeveless dress and a pair of matching ballet-type flats.

Sasha ran her tongue over her lips, tasting coffee. "I slept very well."

"Are you ready to eat breakfast?"

Her fingers curled around his wrists, pulling his

hands away from her face. Sasha didn't trust herself to be that close to Dwight. At least not until she found herself back in control of her runaway senses. He looked, smelled and tasted delicious.

"Yes."

"Do you have a preference?"

Sasha's lips parted as she flashed a wide smile. "I have choices?"

Dwight winked at her. "With me you'll always have choices. I don't believe in all or nothing."

She scrunched up her nose. "Bacon, eggs, toast, juice, coffee and fresh fruit." A beat passed as they stared at each other. "Did I order too much?"

"No, not at all. Do you want to eat inside or out?"

"I'll leave that up to you."

"This weekend is yours, Sasha. I'm your personal genie who will attempt to grant your every wish."

"Outside."

Dwight nodded. "That's what I'd hoped you would say."

"Do you need a sous chef?"

"No. I've got this."

"Kiera told me that you're a very good cook."

"My daughter is biased. My mother is a very good cook. And your mama can also burn some pots. I've been to New Orleans and her gumbo and red beans and rice surpassed any I've eaten there. I'm standing here jawing when I need to feed you."

Sasha took the chair Dwight had vacated. It only took a single glance to see why he'd bought the property. The outdoor kitchen also included a bar, pizza oven and fireplace. Outdoor furniture with all-weather cushions, a rectangular table seating six and two wrought-iron bistro tables, and a quartet of webbed recliners set the stage for casual dining and entertaining. The house and surrounding property was the perfect place in which to retire for someone looking for privacy and solitude.

"I could stay here forever." She sat straight and glanced around her. Sasha did not want to believe she'd spoken her thoughts aloud.

Dwight emerged from the house carrying a large picnic basket with plates, flatware, glasses and foodstuffs he needed to prepare breakfast. He'd made it a practice to use the outdoor kitchen. The exception was inclement weather. Even if temperatures dropped to the forties, he continued to cook outdoors.

Working quickly, he turned on the gas grill, and while the flattop heated, Dwight set the table and put out a covered dish with sliced melon. He'd bought several containers of sliced cantaloupe, honeydew and watermelon. He liked cooking, fishing and dentistry, but not necessarily in that order.

He'd admitted to Sasha that he liked being single; he'd also liked being married. He knew men who remarried within two years after their divorce, and others who'd professed never to marry again. He did not fit in either category. Dwight knew he would've remarried if he had found a woman he loved enough to want her to share his life and his daughter.

Dwight knew Sasha was special, that his feelings for her deepened with each encounter, yet he had no inkling how she felt about marriage. She'd admitted marrying a man she didn't love and that was something he couldn't fathom. If she wasn't pregnant, then why did she marry a man she did not love? He'd originally thought it might have been his celebrity status, yet she was also a celebrity in her own right.

They'd promised each other not to talk about their exes, but Dwight knew that couldn't continue if he hoped to have an open, honest and mature relationship with Sasha. Spending time alone at the lake house was key to them determining whether they would continue dating.

"How do you like your eggs?" he asked Sasha after he'd set a bottle of chilled orange juice on the table. Grasping the handle on a pole, he turned it until a white umbrella opened to shield the table from the intensifying rays of the sun rising higher in the sky.

She shielded her eyes with her hand when she looked up at him. "Scrambled."

Reaching down, Dwight eased her up from the chair. "Come sit under the umbrella. I hope you put on sunblock if you plan to sit outside or you're going to end up looking like a cooked lobster."

"I did apply sunblock, Dr. Adams."

A slight frown furrowed his forehead. He'd told her not to address him as Dr. Adams. "Did you bring a swimsuit?"

"No. I didn't know I needed to bring one."

He ran a finger down the length of her straight nose. "Remember to bring one the next time you come."

Her pale eyebrows rose slightly. "Will there be a next time, Dwight?"

"That will be your decision, Sasha. The invitation is an open one, so the ball will always be in your court." Not waiting for a comeback, Dwight turned on his heel and returned to the grill.

A short time later, he set a platter with fluffy scrambled eggs, crisp grilled bacon, buttered thick-sliced Texas garlic bread heated on the grill and mugs of steaming coffee on the table. He didn't know why but Dwight found food cooked outdoors always tasted better.

Sasha smiled at him across the table. "I could live like this every day."

Dwight also smiled. Sasha had given him the opening he needed for them to be frank with each other. "Maybe that can become a reality one of these days."

Propping her elbow on the table, Sasha rested her chin on the heel of her hand. "How?"

"We could eventually live together."

Sasha's hand came down as if in slow motion. She looked at Dwight as if he'd suddenly taken leave of his senses. "You're talking about us living together when we haven't even..." Her words trailed off when Dwight leaned forward.

"When we don't even know if we're compatible in bed," he said, completing her sentence while reading her thoughts.

"Yes, Dwight."

"Would you live with me if you found our lovemaking satisfying?"

A gamut of confusing emotions held Sasha captive as she tried understanding why Dwight was talking about them making love and living together when they weren't even friends with benefits. "No, Dwight, I won't live with you."

"Won't or can't?"

"Both."

"Why, Sasha?"

"Because I wouldn't live with you unless we were in love with each other."

"You admit to marrying a man you didn't love, so why not live with one you don't love?"

"I never said I didn't love you."

Dwight reacted to her admission as if he'd been stabbed by a sharp object.

"What did you say?"

A surge of strength came to Sasha she hadn't felt since the time she told Grant their marriage was over and that she'd filed for divorce. "You heard what I said, Dr. Adams."

"Stop calling me that."

"What? Dr. Adams?"

"Yes, dammit!"

"Don't cuss at me, Dwight."

"I'm not cursing at you, Natasha."

"Oh, now it's Natasha." She pressed her lips tightly together. "I tell you that I love you and now you're bent out of shape."

Leaning back in his chair, Dwight pressed his palms together. "I had no idea you felt anything more for me aside from friendship. I'm just shocked and pleased that we share the same feelings."

"You—you love me?"

"I'm falling in love with you."

"Is there a difference, Dwight?"

His expression softened when he smiled. "Yes. There is a big difference. You can love a movie, book or a car. But falling in love goes deeper where you are willing to compromise, make sacrifices and protect those you love unconditionally."

"Why me, Dwight, and not some other woman?"

Sasha could not believe she'd asked him why when it was enough to know that her feelings were reciprocated.

"Why not you, Sasha? Do you think you're unworthy of a man's love?"

"Grant felt me unworthy of being his wife. I'd just come off the cupcake competition, and although my team didn't win, I'd become an instant celebrity and attracted a lot of attention because of my hair and laugh. Grant came into the shop where I was working, and he turned on his country-boy charm. He came back a few days later and asked me out. I didn't want to believe that one of Nashville's fastest-rising stars was interested in me. We dated and it wasn't until after I became Mrs. Natasha Manning-Richards that I discovered he married me because he felt we would make the perfect celebrity couple. Once his publicist branded us as the Cowboy and the Redhead, the paparazzi began following us relentlessly. It was only when my star as a pastry chef began to rise that Grant showed his true colors when he attempted to sabotage my career. He insisted I tour with him and accompany him to the studio for recording sessions—time I needed to devote to baking."

Pushing to his feet, Dwight came around the table and sat next to her. "You didn't realize the man was as insecure and controlling as he was talented."

"It wasn't until I'd filed for divorce that my lawyer made me aware of that. The final straw was when he went on tour and left one of his security people at the house to watch me. I knew I'd become a prisoner. That's when I discovered he was tracking my cell phone and had installed cameras throughout the house to monitor my comings and goings. It took all my resolve not to expose him to the tabloids. He finally agreed to end the marriage when I did threaten to talk to a reporter. Grant had me sign a prenup citing I wasn't entitled to any of his earnings or property."

"You'd signed it?"

"Yes. What my dear husband didn't know was that he'd married a woman who didn't need his money."

Sasha knew what she was about to tell Dwight would probably shock him. "I left The Falls two months after graduating to accept a job in Tennessee. Mrs. Harvey, a childless former English teacher, sold the mansion where she'd lived with her late husband, moved into a smaller three-bedroom house in a gated community and advertised for a live-in companion. We bonded and I'd become the granddaughter she never had. Her library was filled with the classics, and because of the onset of senility and failing eyesight, she wanted me to read to her. That's when I fell in love with Dickens, Dumas, Shakespeare, Austen and Brontë. Just before she was confined to an assisted living facility, she asked me what I wanted for my future. And when I told her I wanted to become a pastry chef, she made it happen. Her wealth manager gave me a check to cover my tuition at The Art Institute of Tennessee in Nashville and to rent an apartment. Going to school in Nashville allowed me to visit Mrs. Harvey, although she no longer knew who I was. I'd just received my degree in baking and pastry when I got a call from Mrs. Harvey's lawyer that she'd passed away and I was to attend the reading of her will. She'd left me enough money that it could take me into retirement if I didn't squander it."

"So, it's not that you don't have enough money to keep the bakeshop viable, but whether the business can sustain itself."

"Exactly," she agreed. "I invested my inheritance in an account Grant knew nothing about. I also signed a nondisclosure not to reveal anything about our marriage."

Dwight pulled her closer. "Thank goodness you don't have to deal with that clown anymore."

Sasha rested her head on Dwight's shoulder. "You're right about that. I just can't believe I put up with him for five years before I came to my senses. I didn't fight with Grant because I didn't want to relive my parents' marriage. It's sad when your childhood memories are filled with your mother and father's constant bickering. One time I asked my mother why she didn't leave my father and she said she couldn't because she loved him."

Dwight ran his fingers under the wealth of thick red curls on Sasha's neck. "People fall in love for different reasons."

"You're right, Dwight. I knew you were special the night I came to your house to return Kiera's cell phone. When you gave me your jacket, I decided then you were special. And when you invited me to be your date for the chamber fund-raiser, I felt like the princess in a fairy tale who'd met her prince where they would live happily ever after. I haven't had a lot of experience with men, but those I've met always wanted something from me. You're the only one who wants me for me even though I'm a freckle-faced country girl."

"I don't think you realize how easy it is for me to love you. And there's no need to be self-deprecating because you're one of a kind."

Turning her head, she smiled at him. "I could say the same about you, darling. You're unlike any other man I've met or known."

"So, I'm your darling?" he asked, deadpan.

"You didn't know?"

Dwight smiled. "I didn't want to be presumptuous."

"You are my love, my darling and of course my sweetie."

Dwight pressed his mouth to hers. "How do you taste, Miss Sasha's Sweet Shoppe?"

"I don't know," she whispered. "However, I'm not opposed to offering you a little sample."

Throwing back his head, Dwight laughed loudly, startling a few birds perched in a nearby tree. "What if I want more than just a sample?"

Shifting, Sasha straddled his lap and buried her face against the column of his neck. "Don't you want to find out if you like the sample before you ask for a larger piece?"

Dwight gasped when he felt the press of her bottom as she gyrated against his crotch. He'd hardened so quickly he feared ejaculating before he could make love to her. "Don't! Please." He was pleading with her to stop and didn't care if Sasha knew the power she yielded at that moment.

Her response was to press her breasts against his chest as her hot, moist breath feathered in his ear. "What do you want, Dwight?"

He gasped again as one hand searched under the tank top, fingernails trailing over his breasts. "You, babe."

"How much do you want me?" she taunted.

Dwight had had enough teasing. Wrapping an arm around her waist, he stood up, bringing her up with him. Taking long strides, he managed to slide back the screen, walk into the house and shut it after him without dropping Sasha. He did not want to believe, and was pleasantly surprised, that Sasha was a seductive temptress under the prim and shy exterior he'd come to know. When he'd invited her to spend the weekend with him, his intent wasn't to make love with her, but to give her time to relax and rejuvenate from her hectic week.

He carried her into his bedroom and placed her on the bed. He drew the drapes and then returned to the bed and the drawer in the nightstand to take out a condom. What he and Sasha were about to share was too new for them to risk an unplanned pregnancy. Dwight smiled at Sasha staring up at him when he caught the hem of his tank top and pulled it up and over his head. His eyes searched her face for a hint of uncertainty but saw only confidence in the green eyes. Dwight took his time undressing, and when he was completely nude, he saw Sasha's expression change as her lips parted.

Sasha tried not to react to seeing Dwight's nakedness, but she couldn't believe that his body was as magnificent as his face. Lean and muscled, he was Michelangelo's *David* in mahogany instead of marble. She forced herself not to look at his erection when he slipped on the condom. Sitting up, she slipped the straps to the dress off her shoulders, baring her breasts. Dwight got into bed with her and kissed her as he removed the dress and underwear. Her mouth was as busy as Dwight's, slanting across his lips, jaw and ear. Her teeth nibbled at his exposed throat, staking her claim at the same time a deep moan rose from the valley of his wide chest.

Dwight wanted to take Sasha hard and fast because he had been celibate much too long—but he decided not to. She needed to be loved, to know that she was loved. Cradling her head in his hands, he increased the pressure of his mouth on hers until her lips parted and he took possession of her tongue. One hand moved from her head to a satiny shoulder and still farther to a firm breast. It filled his hand, the nipple tightening against his palm. His thumb drew circles around the areola, pebbling and increasing his own desire and arousal.

Shifting slightly, he raised his body, while hers writhed with an escalating awakening. Slowly, methodically, Dwight held her hands at her sides while he slipped down the length of her silken body until his face was level with the juncture of her thighs. The erotic essence of her body filled his nostrils when he buried his face against the silky down concealing her femininity. His hot breath seared her delicate flesh before it cooled with the sweep of his moist tongue.

Sasha wanted to tell Dwight to stop yet couldn't. Not when his rapacious tongue made every nerve in her body seem to be on fire; not when she felt herself falling over the edge where orgasms waited for her. Waves of ecstasy throbbed through her body. She gasped in sweet agony, and her fingers tightened on the sheet, twisting and pulling it from the confines of the mattress. She breathed in deep, soul-drenching drafts at the same time ripples of fulfillment gripped her. Arching, unashamed screams exploded from her parted lips as she gave herself up to the passion hurtling her higher than she had ever soared before.

The pulsating continued, faster and stronger until she abandoned herself to the liquid fire sweeping her into a vortex of sweet, burning fulfillment. The flames of passion had not subsided entirely when she felt Dwight's erection easing into her. She took him in, inch by inch. He moaned as if in pain, then began a slow thrusting, preparing her body to accept all of him.

Sasha moaned, her body opening and giving Dwight the advantage he needed as he rolled his hips, burying himself to the root of his penis. Her hot, wet flesh closed around him like a tight glove, and he knew it was helpless to hold back any longer. He rolled his hips again, each thrust deeper, harder. The sensation of her body opening and closing around him, pulling him in where he did not know where he began and Sasha ended, hurled him to a dimension he did not know existed. He had to let go of his damned passions.

Sasha's soft sighs of satisfaction were his undoing. Listening to the throaty moans from her forced him to release the obdurate control on the passions he had kept in check and withheld from every woman since his divorce. Collapsing heavily on her slender body, he sucked in precious air to fill his lungs with much-needed oxygen. Dwight didn't know where he found the strength, but he managed to roll off Sasha's body, while at the same time savoring the pulsing aftermath of his own release.

The bedroom was silent as they lay side by side, eyes closed. Sasha reached for his hand, threading their fingers together. There was no need for conversation. Their bodies had spoken for them. She loved him and he loved her.

Chapter Eleven

Sasha did not want to believe life could be so perfect starting with the weekend at the lake house. She and Dwight spent more time in bed than out, talking and making endless love. He told her about his forensic psychologist FBI special-agent father, who lost his life when the driver of a tractor trailer had fallen asleep behind the wheel and plowed into his car.

He'd also disclosed that he might have contributed to the dissolution of his marriage; although he had not accepted a ROTC Guard/Reserves scholarship, he owed the army six years with two years remaining on active duty. He'd elected to fulfill the two-year commitment before enrolling in dental school, unaware that Adrienne was pregnant. He hadn't been there for her during the first year of Kiera's life; then he was gone again after he'd enrolled in dental school. Most of her immediate family had left The Falls, and Adrienne had made up her mind that she also didn't want to stay.

It wasn't until mid-June when Sasha was finally able to hire an assistant, a young man who was extremely talented. She suspected he was attracted to Kiera, who totally ignored him, and Sasha had come to believe Kiera resented his intrusion because it reduced the time they would spend together. With the additional help, she was able to fulfill more special orders from clients as far away as Beckley.

Her alone time with Dwight was infrequent because they were unable to get away to the lake more than once a month. Most of the time Kiera accompanied them, and the weekend before Kiera left to go to New York to vacation with her mother, Victoria and Charlotte also joined them. Kiera passed her driver's test, and Dwight had promised that when she returned in August they would go shopping for a late-model used car.

Sasha had just parked the van at her home when the front door opened, and her mother walked out onto the porch. Charlotte was now an official member of the Ladies Auxiliary, which was on hiatus until the fall, and she was looking forward to the induction ceremony. Charlotte's strained expression said it all: she was upset. Reaching for her tote, she got out, her pulse throbbing at the base of her throat.

"What's the matter, Mama?" She prayed her mother wasn't experiencing chest pains again. Reaching for her hands, she discovered they were ice-cold.

"I just got a call from Grant Richards."

"What the hell…?" Sasha paused, taking a deep

breath. "I'm sorry about that." She didn't want her mother to bear the brunt of her anger. "Why would he be calling you?" She knew there was no way he was able to call her because she'd changed her cell's number.

"I suppose he still has my number from when he came here for your daddy's funeral."

"What does he want, Mama?"

"He said he has upcoming concerts beginning next month in Charleston, Richmond, Virginia, and the DC area, and he wants to see you. He did ask for your number, but I know you don't want him to have it."

Sasha struggled to control her anger. "Not only don't I want to talk to him, but I also don't want to ever see him again."

"He did say he was sorry for how he treated you."

"And you believed him?"

A pained expression flitted over Charlotte's features. "He did sound remorseful."

"That's because he's a charlatan and a con man, Mama. He knows what to say to draw you in, and then before you know it, he's got you trapped in his web where he'll control every phase of your life."

"I thought by this time you would've forgiven him. It's not good to carry around so much hate."

Sasha threw up her hands. "I'm sorry, Mama, but I'm not you. You were a sponge, soaking up everything Daddy dumped on you and still you turned the other cheek."

Charlotte's eyes filled with tears. "That's not fair."

"What's not fair is becoming a receptacle for abuse. What really bothers me is that I told you what he did to me and you still want to welcome him into your home like he was the perfect son-in-law."

"Don't put words in my mouth, Natasha. I never said I was going to invite him here, so don't shoot the messenger."

Sasha knew her mother was angry when her face turned beet red. "I think we'd better end this conversation before we say something we'll later regret."

"Yes, we'd better," Charlotte shot back.

"I'm going inside to shower, and then I'm going to bed."

Sasha was still upset when she crawled into bed. She cursed Grant even though she knew he couldn't have done what he did to her if she hadn't given him permission. Too often she'd asked herself when had her ego surpassed her common sense because she'd gotten an A-list recording artist to choose her to become his wife from among the screaming, adoring women who'd risk life and limb to get close enough to touch him.

Her cell phone rang, and she knew from the programmed ringtone that it was Dwight. They'd made plans to go to the lake house after she closed on Saturday now that Kiera was away. She picked up the phone. "Yes."

There was a pregnant pause before Dwight said, "What's the matter?"

"Nothing," she lied smoothly.

"If nothing's wrong, then why does it sound as if you've lost your best friend?"

"Look, Dwight, I just don't feel like talking right now."

"If that's the case, then call me when you're in a better mood."

Suddenly the connection went dead, and she knew he'd hung up on her. Frustrated, Sasha threw the phone across the room, and it landed on the chair in the corner. Hot, angry tears pricked the backs of her eyelids, but she refused to cry. She'd cried enough because of two men to last several lifetimes. First it was because of her father, when she stayed on her young knees praying for him to change; and then it was because of Grant, who had used her to his advantage, then openly flaunted his infidelity with a woman who'd grinned in her face while she was sleeping with her husband. Sasha knew she had to get her head together before seeing Dwight again, because it wasn't fair to him to let her dilemma with Grant destroy her newfound happiness.

Dwight immediately recognized the number on the phone's screen, wondering why his daughter was calling him from the Dominican Republic. He tapped the speaker feature. "What's up, Kiera?"

"Daddy, can you come and get me?"

His stomach muscles tightened as he struggled not to panic. "What's the matter?"

"I was having a conversation with Mom when Omar called me an ungrateful little snot who should be slapped across the mouth after I told him I needed to talk with my mother without his interruptions."

Dwight closed his eyes as he whispered a silent prayer for patience. He did not want to believe the man to whom he'd entrusted his daughter's safety had threatened to hit her. "Put your mother on the phone."

"She went out."

"Then put Omar on the phone."

"He's out, too. I'm alone in the condo."

"Stay there, get your passport and pack your bags,

Kiera. And if your mother says anything, then tell her I'm coming to get you."

"What about Omar?"

"Don't worry about him, Kiera. I'll take care of him when I get there. Keep your phone on and charged in case I have to call you."

"Okay, Daddy. When do you think you'll get here?"

"Hopefully sometime tomorrow. I have to call the airline and see if I can reserve a flight."

Dwight hung up and scrolled through his phone for the number to an airline with departures to Punta Cana. It took him more than forty-five minutes to reserve a seat to the Caribbean island. He was scheduled to board a red-eye in Charleston for Miami, then take a connecting flight to Punta Cana.

He tapped the number to the bakeshop, hoping Sasha was in a better mood than she'd been a couple of days ago. He'd told her to call him, and she hadn't. While he'd been prepared to wait indefinitely, now he owed it to her to let her know he was going out of the country, and he hoped this would be the last time he would have to drop everything to rescue his daughter.

"Sasha's Sweet Shoppe."

Dwight hesitated. He still wasn't used to hearing a masculine voice answer the phone. Sasha's young assistant, Christian Weber, looked more like a male model with sun-streaked shoulder-length twists, a deeply tanned tawny-brown face and a tall, slender body. He'd noticed him staring at his daughter and he'd left it to Sasha to warn him that Kiera was much too young to date a twenty-two-year-old man, and that her father was overly protective of his only child.

"May I please speak to Miss Sasha."

"Miss Sasha is on the other line with a client. Would you like to leave a message?"

"Yes. Please tell her to call Dr. Adams."

"I'll give her the message, Dr. Adams. How's Kiera?"

"Kiera's well," Dwight lied. She wasn't well, and she wouldn't be until he brought her back to Wickham Falls.

"That's good. I know you don't want me to date your daughter but—"

"Look, son," Dwight said, cutting him off. "You and I will have to talk about Kiera when I see you. But right now, I need to speak to Miss Sasha."

"Right. I'll let her know as soon as she hangs up."

Dwight hung up, shaking his head. Right now, he had enough problems with Omar to even think of how to convince the pastry chef that his daughter was unobtainable and unavailable to him.

His focus was on Omar, who allegedly had threatened to hit Kiera. When Adrienne had informed him that she was remarrying, Dwight had been concerned about the man who was to become his daughter's stepfather. However, when he met Omar, the man reassured him that he would love and protect Kiera as if she were his own. Kiera had grown up calling Omar Dad, yet something had to have happened between them for her to refer to him by his given name. Something he knew annoyed the man.

His phone rang and Dwight answered it before the second ring. "Hello."

"This is Miss Sasha from Sasha's Sweet Shoppe returning Dr. Adams's call. Is he available?"

He smiled. The teasing woman with whom he'd fallen in love was back. "This is he. How are you, Miss Sasha?"

"I'm well, thank you. And you?"

Dwight sobered as he focused on why he'd called Sasha. "I have to fly down to the Caribbean to bring Kiera back home."

"She is sick?"

"No. It's more like we're having a family crisis."

"I'm sorry to hear that. When are you leaving?"

"I'm driving up to Charleston in a couple of hours. I plan to check into a hotel to get some sleep before taking a red-eye to Miami for a connecting flight to Punta Cana. I'll book a return flight once I get there."

"Do whatever you have to do to make certain Kiera's okay. Tell her I love and miss her when you see her."

Dwight went completely still. It was the first time Sasha had verbalized her affection for his daughter. "I will."

"I love you, Dwight."

He smiled. "I know that. I love you, too."

"Be safe."

"Thank you. I'll see you when we get back."

Dwight sat in the condo's living room staring at the man he'd expected to love and protect his daughter as her stepfather. By the time the jet had touched down at the Punta Cana airport, Dwight had become even more resolute that this would be the last time he would have to drop everything to extract Kiera from a hostile family confrontation.

He leaned forward, impaling the shorter, slightly built man with a long, penetrating direct stare. "When you married Adrienne, you promised me you would care for and protect Kiera as if she was your daughter. Now I hear you want to slap her across the mouth."

Omar ran a hand over his shaved light brown pate at the same time he forced what could pass for a smile. Omar Johnson had earned a reputation as a brilliant litigator, and when he graduated at the top of his law school class, prestigious law firms were lining up with lucrative offers to entice him to join them. As the CFO of a Fortune 500 company, Adrienne and Omar had become a super couple. They had a condo in a luxury Manhattan high-rise and the condo in the Caribbean with breathtaking views of the sea.

"I really wouldn't have hit her, Dwight."

"I'd hope you wouldn't because then I would have to get involved. And I can promise you, man-to-man, that it would be more than a slap that I'd inflict on you."

Omar's light brown eyes grew wider. "Are you threatening me, Dwight?"

"No. I don't have to do that because I'm taking my daughter home with me, and this will be the last time she will go anywhere with you."

"Have you forgotten I'm Adrienne's husband? There will be times when we'll have to be together."

"No, I haven't forgotten. What I want you to remember is Kiera's old enough to decide if she doesn't want to see you or her mother. And because I'm legally responsible for *my daughter*, I have the final say on what she can and cannot go or do."

"Kiera is not only your child, Dwight. She does have a mother."

Dwight's hands curled into fists. Only his military training kept him from leaping across the room and choking the pompous little man. "And you've been married to Adrienne long enough to have fathered a few kids of your own, so you can be a real dad and slap them in the mouth." He realized he'd hit a sore spot when Omar recoiled from the gibe.

"Daddy, I'm ready to leave."

He stood up when Kiera walked into the living room pulling two wheeled bags. "Do you have your passport?"

Kiera patted the cross-body bag slung across her chest. "It's in here."

Dwight picked up his carry-on, walked over to the door, opened it and let Kiera precede him out into the hallway. He didn't get to see Adrienne, who'd remained in her bedroom during his brief visit. When she'd returned his call, she claimed she did not have a problem with Dwight coming to get their daughter. There was something in her voice indicating relief that Kiera would be leaving.

He punched a button for the elevator. Dwight had hired a driver to take them to the airport for a flight back to the States. They had a three-hour layover in Miami before flying on to Charleston, West Virginia, where he would pick up the Jeep from airport parking.

"I think Mom and Omar are getting a divorce."

"That happens with married couples." Dwight had no intention of getting involved in his ex-wife's marriage.

"It doesn't bother you, Daddy?"

He gave Kiera a direct stare. "No. Your mother and her husband are adults who must work through their own issues. It's only when you're drawn into it that I get involved."

Kiera's eyelids fluttered. "They fight all the time, and I was sick of it. I really don't want to be with them ever again."

"You don't have to worry about that right now.

Maybe once they work through their problems, you may change your mind." Dwight didn't want Kiera not to have a relationship with her mother, but it was incumbent on Adrienne to stabilize her marriage or lose her daughter.

The elevator arrived and they stepped into the car. The doors closed and it descended quickly to the lobby. Tropical heat enveloped them as the automatic doors opened. Dwight's driver alighted from the air-cooled sedan parked near the entrance to the building and took their bags.

Dwight sat in the rear of the car with Kiera and stared out the side window. Under another set of circumstances, he would've enjoyed an extended stay in the beautiful tropical island. He was still smarting from Omar believing he had some legal claim on Kiera because he was married to her mother.

Stretching out his legs, he folded his arms over his chest and closed his eyes. He was leaving Punta Cana to return to Wickham Falls and Sasha. He'd thought a lot about her during his stay, and the depth of his feelings for Sasha shocked him. Dwight realized they had reached a point where their relationship had to be resolved with permanence.

Sasha walked out of the kitchen when she heard the doorbell. Charlotte had gone out and she was alone in the house. She opened the door and felt her legs buckle slightly when she stared at the man she'd believed she would never see again.

"What are you doing here?"

He smiled and laugh lines fanned out around the

large hazel eyes with lashes women paid a lot of money to affect. "What? No 'hello, Grant'?"

Sasha's eyes narrowed. "You didn't answer my question. What are you doing here?"

Grant Richards ran his fingers through thick wavy brown hair. "May I come in?"

She glanced around him to see if he'd come with someone, but there was a lone pickup parked in front of the house. "No." Sasha opened the door wider and stepped out on the porch.

Grant stared at her bare feet. "You still don't like to wear shoes."

Leaning against the door frame, she crossed her arms under her breasts. "I know you didn't come here to talk about my feet. Say what you have to say, Grant. I am busy."

"How's the bakeshop?"

Sasha was quickly losing her patience with the man who'd made her life a living hell. She lowered her arms. "Goodbye, Grant."

He caught her upper arm. "Don't go, Sasha. I came to tell you that this will be my last tour."

She stared at the tanned hand on her arm until he released her. "What you do with your life is your business."

Grant's shoulders slumped under the untucked white shirt he'd paired with well-worn jeans and his signature black snakeskin boots. "This will be my last tour because I've been diagnosed with the onset of ALS. Earlier this year I woke up and found it hard to even walk to make it to the bathroom. At first I thought it was muscle cramps, so I applied ice and then heat, and when they went away, I forgot about it. Then a couple of months later I experienced weakness in my right hand and again I ignored it. The day after I signed up for the upcoming tour, I tripped and fell and ended up in the hospital for a battery of tests. That's when I was told I had ALS."

Sasha couldn't believe what she was hearing. "You have ALS and you're still going on the tour?"

"Yes. Instead of singing, playing guitar, while dancing around the stage, I'm going to sit on a stool and just sing. I'll explain to everyone when the show opens that I had an accident and hurt my legs and back, so they're going to get to see a very different Grant Richards."

"I don't understand, Grant. Why aren't you taking care of yourself? What if you fall and seriously injure yourself?"

He angled his head. "That's a chance I'll have to take. I want to go out while I'm still on top." He sobered quickly, shocking Sasha when his eyes filled with tears. "I really came here to apologize, and I'm ashamed of what I did to you."

She averted her head because it pained her to see him cry. "I'm over it, Grant. I've moved on with my life."

"But I can't move on with mine until you forgive me."

Her gaze swung back to him. "You want me to give you absolution?" Sasha's heart turned over when tears streamed down his face. She never would've believed the narcissistic man who never gave a whit for anything or anyone but himself was asking for forgiveness.

She knew it took a lot of strength and courage for Grant to come to her when he knew his days were numbered by a disease that would eventually confine him to a wheelchair before it claimed his life.

Taking a step, she wrapped her arms around his waist and rested her forehead on his shoulder. "I forgive you, Grant," she said.

Grant cupped her chin in his hand, lowered his head and brushed a kiss across her parted lips. "Thank you, baby."

Sasha reached up and blotted his tears with her fingertips. "You take care of yourself."

He nodded. "Now I don't have a choice. No more chasing women and all-night parties."

"Do you have someone who will take care of you?"

"My mother. She's the only one who knows besides you and my manager. After this tour, the world will know the whole story. I'd like you to keep this between us until my manager makes the announcement."

"Okay, Grant," she promised.

He gave her a weak smile. "You take care of yourself. And make sure the next man you take up with will appreciate everything you have to offer him. It wasn't until you left me that I realized you were one badass woman, and you were the better half of the Cowboy and the Redhead."

Turning on his heel, Grant walked off the porch and got into the pickup. Sasha didn't wait to see him drive off. She also didn't see the man sitting across the street in the Jeep watching the interaction with her ex-husband.

Chapter Twelve

Dwight didn't want to believe what he'd just witnessed. He'd come to Sasha's house to talk about wanting to marry her; however, it appeared as if she was still involved with her ex-husband as evidenced by the kiss they'd shared. He wondered if she'd made up the story about his controlling her life when they were married to elicit sympathy as the victim or maybe to shift the blame from herself to him because she'd been the villainess.

He started the Jeep and headed back to the main road, wondering why he'd always chosen the wrong woman to give his heart to. When he slipped an engagement and then a wedding ring on Adrienne's hand, Dwight had believed it would be forever. However, forever ended when she decided to marry the man with whom she'd had an affair while she and Dwight were engaged.

It had become an instant rerun with Sasha. She'd married and divorced Grant Richards, labeling him a monster and saying she never wanted to see him again, yet she couldn't resist locking lips with him on the porch of her home, where anyone walking or driving by could see them.

Perhaps, Dwight mused, he was destined to remain single. Not being committed to a woman and living his life by his leave was satisfying and uncomplicated. His only responsibility was Kiera and planning for her future.

He drove aimlessly until he found himself pulling into a parking space at the Wolf Den. It was Military Monday and there was always a steady stream of active and former military coming and going. He walked into the sports bar, waiting for his eyes to adjust to the dimmer light, and took a seat at the bar. The lunchtime crowd was gone and there were quite a few empty tables and booths.

Aiden Gibson came from the back carrying a keg of beer. He set the keg on the floor and extended his hand. "Welcome back, stranger. How long has it been?"

Dwight shook Aiden's hand. "It's been a while."

"A while? The last time I remember you coming in was with a redhead who bakes the most incredible cakes that we sell out of them whenever they're listed on the chalkboard with the day's special." Aiden paused to hook up the keg. "What are you drinking?"

"I'll take anything you have on tap."

Aiden picked up a mug, tilted it and filled it with a golden foaming liquid, and then set it on a coaster. "Why do you look so down in the dumps?"

Picking up the mug, Dwight took a long swallow. "Do I?"

"Hell, yeah, you do," Aiden countered. "I'm willing to bet that it has something to do with a woman.

Sasha?" he asked when Dwight did not deny or confirm his assumption.

"Women," Dwight said under his breath. "Can't live with them and can't live without them."

Resting his elbows on the bar, Aiden leaned forward. "You seem to have done quite well as a bachelor."

Dwight's dark eyes met Aiden's blue-green ones. "True, but things change when you meet someone you really care about."

"I know what you mean, buddy. I thought I'd never fall in love again until I met Taryn. Even though she is an amazing woman and mother, it's not all sunshine and butterflies. Every once in a while we have our ups and downs, but it only makes our marriage stronger."

Dwight took another sip of the cold brew. "You're preaching to the choir, Aiden."

"If you know, then why the long face, Dwight?"

"It gets a little sticky when there's a third person in the relationship." There was no way he was going to tell Aiden that he saw Sasha kissing her ex-husband.

Aiden grimaced. "That does make it a little messy."

"I can think of another word to describe it. Enough talk about me. How are your kids?"

"They're all good. Taryn is still homeschooling the girls until they get to middle school, while Daniel believes all he has to do is scream to get what he wants."

"How old is he now?"

"Two."

Dwight smiled. "There's a reason why they're called the Terrible Twos."

"Didn't your daughter graduate this year?"

"No. She still has another year." He had a Wednesday morning appointment with a dealer in Beckley to purchase a car for Kiera. He'd asked the dealer to order the same make and model, but a different color, as the one Victoria drove. Kiera was anticipating getting the car a week before the start of the new school year, and he knew she would be surprised when it arrived earlier.

Dwight picked up a menu and ordered the daily special of baked chicken, garlic mashed potatoes, roasted asparagus and corn bread, along with another glass of beer. He made it home to find Kiera in his kitchen sitting on a stool between Sasha and her grandmother.

Kiera jumped and came over to hug him. "Hi, Daddy. We were waiting for you to come back so we can all eat together at Ruthie's."

Smiling, he dropped a kiss on Kiera's chemically relaxed hair. She'd taken out the braids and had the stylist relax her thick natural hair, set it on large rollers and trim the ends. Using a round brush and blow-dryer, she blew it out until it hung in stick-straight strands halfway down her back.

"I'm going to have to take a rain check, sweetie. I already ate at the Wolf Den."

Sasha swiveled on the stool. "You went to the Den without me?"

Dwight stared at the woman he wanted to hate for her duplicity yet couldn't because he'd found himself in too deep. "Sasha, will you please step out on the porch with me? I'd like to talk to you about something."

"Are you going to ask her to marry you?" Kiera asked in a loud voice.

"Kiera Robyn Adams, mind your manners!" Victoria scolded. "How many times have I warned you to stay out of grown folks' business?"

Kiera lowered her eyes. "Sorry, Grammie."

"It's your father and Sasha you should be apologizing to."

"I'm sorry, Daddy. Miss Sasha."

Dwight nodded to Kiera. "Apology accepted."

Sasha slipped off the stool and came over to him. "I'm ready to talk whenever you are."

Cupping her elbow, he escorted her out of the house and onto the porch. Dwight waited for Sasha to sit on the cushioned love seat before dropping down beside her. "Is there something you want to tell me?"

Shifting, Sasha turned to look directly at him. "What's going on, Dwight?"

He blinked slowly. "That's what I want to know, Sasha. What's up with you and your ex-husband?"

"Say what?"

"Say what," he repeated. "I came by to see you earlier this afternoon, and to say I was shocked is an understatement when I saw you locking lips with Grant Richards. I thought you never wanted to see him again. What's next, Sasha? A reconciliation?"

"It's not what you think!"

"No, Sasha. It's not what I think but what I saw."

"What you saw is not what you think, Dwight."

He closed his eyes. "Please don't tell me what I think. Right now, my thoughts are saying that I don't trust you. And I've made it a practice not to deal with women I can't trust."

"I want you to trust me when I say I can't tell you why Grant came to see me and why he kissed me."

"Can't or won't?"

"I can't. At least not now."

Dwight extended his legs, crossing his feet at the ankles. He knew what he was going to tell Sasha would forever affect their relationship. "I think we should stop seeing each other until you can be truthful with me. Meanwhile, feel free to date other people." He pushed off the love seat. "Please excuse me. I'm going inside."

Sasha sat, numbed by what had just transpired between her and Dwight. He had just broken up with her. She had no idea he had seen her with Grant, and she'd promised her ex-husband that she wouldn't say anything about his physical condition.

She wanted to keep Grant's secret, and she wanted to keep her man. This was the second time Grant wanted her to shield him from the public. The first was the non disclosure when she was legally bound not to reveal the details of their marriage. Now he'd asked her not to talk about a disease that would eventually rob him of the ability to walk, talk, feed or relieve himself.

Pulling her legs up and tucking them under her body, she closed her eyes and pressed her head against the back cushion. She'd walked away from Grant to start over, and when she least expected it, he'd walked back into her life to control her once again. When she'd opened the door to find him standing on her porch, her impulse was to close it and leave him standing there. Even before he'd revealed his diagnosis, she'd noticed the slight trembling in his right hand—something she didn't remember when they lived together. He would periodically complain of fatigue, which she attributed to nonstop touring and too many late-night parties.

Sasha opened her eyes and smiled. She wasn't ready to give up Dwight Adams, not when she'd waited all her life to find a man who loved her for herself and not what she could do to enhance his life or image. Dwight lived and worked in Wickham Falls, which meant he wasn't going anywhere, and neither was she. She returned to the kitchen, smiling. "It looks like it's just us ladies tonight."

Victoria walked over to her and placed her hand on Sasha's arm. "Are you all right?"

"Of course. Why would you think I'm not?"

The sweep hand on the wall clock made a full revolution before Victoria smiled. "Nothing. We can leave as soon as I get my bag."

Dwight stood up when he heard the approaching car. This was the second time Kiera had broken curfew. He'd given her the car a month ago, and during that time he rarely saw her when she didn't have classes or work at the bakeshop. He'd warned her the next time she came in after midnight she would forfeit her right to drive the car for a month. He watched her as she got out and then stopped when she saw him leaning over the railing to the porch.

"I'm sorry, Daddy, that I'm late but I had to drop my friend off home. We had to wait before we could get a lane at the bowling alley."

"Where does your friend live, Kiera Adams?"

"Mineral Springs."

"Is this friend a girl or a boy?"

Kiera placed her foot on the first step. "It's a boy but I swear I'm not doing anything with him."

"Are you dating this boy?"

Kiera took another step. "Not really."

"Either you are, or you aren't."

"We've seen each other a few times."

"You're dating a boy from another town and not once did you think of bringing him home so I could meet him." Dwight didn't want to tell his daughter most kids from The Falls did not date kids who lived in the Springs because of a football rivalry going back at least a couple of generations.

"Miss Sasha met him."

"You introduced your boyfriend to your boss and not your father." Dwight had not seen or heard from Sasha since the day he confronted her about her ex-husband.

"Miss Sasha is like a mom and I wanted her to let me know if she liked Enrique."

"Miss Sasha isn't your mom, Kiera."

"I know, but she could be my stepmother if you married her. Why did you stop dating her, Daddy?"

Dwight held out his hand and Kiera dropped the car fob on his outstretched palm. He had no intention of discussing his relationship with Sasha with her. "You'll get this back when I get to meet the boy who's responsible for your breaking curfew and losing your driving privileges."

Kiera stomped up the steps and went into the house, slamming the door behind her. His daughter mentioning Sasha was a reminder of how long it had been since he last saw her. Dwight knew he was being a hardnose, because he didn't want a repeat with her of what he'd had with Adrienne.

He went inside and flopped down on a chair in the family room. Being a parent was hard. Being the parent to a teenager was trial by fire. Dwight picked up the remote device and flicked on the television, channel surfing until he found a show featuring entertainment news.

He sat straight up, his eyes glued to Grant Richards's image when it filled the screen. The man was chairing a news conference in which he was announcing his retirement from the music scene. Dwight did not want to believe what he was hearing. Grant had been diagnosed with ALS, and he had sworn his mother, manager and ex-wife to secrecy that they would not reveal the debilitating disease until after he completed his last tour because he did not want to disappoint his loyal fans.

Dwight buried his face in his hands. When he'd asked Sasha to tell him about the encounter with her ex, she said, *I can't. At least not now.* He didn't want to believe he'd lost the woman who'd made him plan for the next day and years to come.

He knew it was late, but he was past caring. He had to know if he had a second chance to make things right. Picking up the phone on the side table, Dwight tapped Sasha's number.

"Hello."

He knew he'd woken her. "Sasha."

"Yes, Dwight."

"Can you forgive me for being a selfish, jealous fool?"

"There's nothing to forgive, darling. I know you had a right to feel the way you did, but I'd promised Grant that I wouldn't tell anyone about his condition because it wasn't mine to tell."

"I know that now."

"Dwight?"

"What, babe?"

"I love you so much."

"I love you more. Can you do me a favor?"

"What?" she asked.

"Will you marry me?"

Sasha's distinctive laugh came through the earpiece. "I thought you'd never ask."

"Is that a yes or no, Miss Manning?"

"Of course it's a yes, Dr. Adams."

"What size ring do you wear?"

"A six."

"Tomorrow we'll go ring shopping before we officially announce our engagement."

Sasha laughed again. "Do you want a long engagement?"

"No. Do you want children?" he asked.

"We already have a daughter, so a son would be nice."

Dwight hadn't thought about fathering more children until he fell in love with Sasha. And if they did have a child together, it would be raised as an only child because Kiera would be so much older than her sister or brother.

"When do you want to start trying for a baby?"

"Tomorrow. And I've always wanted a Christmas wedding."

It was August and if Sasha got pregnant right away then she would be at least three months along by the end of the year. "Are you sure you want to walk down the aisle with a belly?"

"Yes. As long as it's your baby in my belly."

"You keep talking like that and I'm going to come over there and take you to a motel where we can make up for lost time."

"Come on over, darling. I'll be waiting on the porch when you get here."

Six Months Later...

Sasha walked out of the bathroom, her eyes meeting her husband's. What she'd expected was confirmed. She was pregnant. They'd been trying for a baby since the day before he slipped a ring on her finger, but with no results. They'd exchanged vows during a winter wonderland–themed wedding in the barn behind the

Wolf Den. Her brothers and their families had come in for the event, and she and Dwight took a weeklong honeymoon on St. Thomas, returning more in love than when they left the States. Kiera hadn't changed her mind about becoming a professional chef when she'd sent off applications to top culinary schools.

Dwight pushed into a sitting position as he looked at her. "Why are you smiling?"

Sasha slipped into bed next to him. "You did it. We're pregnant."

Throwing back his head, Dwight howled like a wolf. "Congratulations, Mama!"

Straddling his lap, she pressed her breasts to his bare chest. "Congratulations to you, too, Daddy!"

Sasha could not believe all her dreams had come true. She'd married a man she loved, she was carrying his baby and she could claim an incredible stepdaughter and mother-in-law. And Sasha's Sweet Shoppe had earned the reputation of offering some of the best desserts in Johnson County.

* * * * *

We've got some exciting changes coming in our February 2020 Special Edition books!

Our covers have been redesigned, and the emotional contemporary romances from your favorite authors will be longer in length.

Be sure to come back next month for more great stories from Special Edition!

YOU HAVE
JUST READ A
HARLEQUIN®
SPECIAL
EDITION
BOOK.

Discover more heartfelt tales of **family, friendship** and **love** from the Harlequin Special Edition series. Be sure to look for all six Harlequin® Special Edition books every month.

⬧ HARLEQUIN®
SPECIAL EDITION

AVAILABLE THIS MONTH FROM
Harlequin® Special Edition

FORTUNE'S FRESH START
The Fortunes of Texas: Rambling Rose • by Michelle Major

In the small Texas burg of Rambling Rose, real estate investor Callum Fortune is making a big splash. The last thing he needs is any personal complications slowing his pace—least of all nurse Becky Averill, a beautiful widow with twin baby girls!

HER RIGHT-HAND COWBOY
Forever, Texas • by Marie Ferrarella

A clause in her father's will requires Ena O'Rourke to work the family ranch for six months before she can sell it. She's livid at her father throwing a wrench in her life from beyond the grave. But Mitch Randall, foreman of the Double E, is always there for her. As Ena spends more time on the ranch—and with Mitch—new memories are laid over the old...and perhaps new opportunities to make a life.

SECOND-CHANCE SWEET SHOP
Wickham Falls Weddings • by Rochelle Alers

Brand-new bakery owner Sasha Manning didn't anticipate that the teenager she hired would have a father more delectable than anything in her shop window! Sasha still smarts from falling for a man too good to be true. Divorced single dad Dwight Adams will have to prove to Sasha that he's the real deal and not a wolf in sheep's clothing...and learn to trust someone with his heart along the way.

COOKING UP ROMANCE
The Taylor Triplets • by Lynne Marshall

Lacy was a redhead with a pink food truck who prepared mouthwatering meals. Hunky construction manager Zack Gardner agreed to let her feed his hungry crew in exchange for cooking lessons for his young daughter. But it looked like the lovely businesswoman was transforming the single dad's life in more ways than one—since a family secret is going to change both of their lives in ways they never expected.

RELUCTANT HOMETOWN HERO
Wildfire Ridge • by Heatherly Bell

Former army officer Ryan Davis doesn't relish the high-profile role of town sheriff, but when duty calls, he responds. Even if it means helping animal rescuer Zoey Castillo find her missing foster dog. When Ryan asks her out, Zoey is wary of a relationship in the spotlight—especially given her past. If the sheriff wants to date her, he'll have to prove that two legs are better than four.

THE WEDDING TRUCE
Something True • by Kerri Carpenter

For the sake of their best friends' wedding, divorce attorney Xander Ryan and wedding planner Grace Harris are calling a truce. Now they must plan the perfect wedding shower together. But Xander doesn't believe in marriage! And Grace believes in romance and true love. Clearly, they have nothing in common. In fact, all Xander feels when Grace is near is disdain and...desire. Wait. What?

Mackenzie Wallace is back and wants excitement with her old crush. She hopes there's still some bad boy lurking beneath the single father's upright exterior. Dan Adams isn't the boy he was—but secrets from his past might still manage to keep them apart.

Read on for a sneak preview of the next book in the Gallant Lake Stories series,
Her Homecoming Wish,
by Jo McNally.

"There's an open bottle of very expensive scotch on the counter, just waiting for someone to enjoy it." She laughed again, softly this time. "And I'd *really* like to hear the story of how Danger Dan turned into a lawman."

Dan grimaced. He hated that stupid nickname Ryan had made up, even if he *had* earned it back then. Especially coming from Mack.

"Is your husband waiting upstairs?" Dan wasn't sure where that question came from, but, to be fair, all Mack had ever talked about was leaving Gallant Lake, having a big wedding and a bigger house. The girl had goals, and from what he'd heard, she'd reached every one of them.

"I don't have a husband anymore." She brushed past him and headed toward the counter. "So are you joining me or not?"

Dan glanced at his watch, not sure how to digest that information. "I'm off duty in fifteen minutes."

Her long hair swung back and forth as she walked ahead of him. So did her hips. *Damn.*

"And you're all about following the rules now? You really have changed, haven't you? Pity. I guess I'm drinking my first glass alone. You'll just have to catch up."

He frowned. Mackenzie had been strong-willed, but never sassy. Never the type to sneak into her father's store alone for an after-hours drink. Not the type to taunt him. Not the type to break the rules.

Looked like he wasn't the only one who'd changed since high school.

Don't miss
Her Homecoming Wish *by Jo McNally,*
available February 2020 wherever
Harlequin® Special Edition books and ebooks are sold.

Harlequin.com